COWBOY STOLEN KISS FOR CHRISTMAS

A Very Country Christmas Wish #8

JO GRAFFORD

Copyright © 2024 by Jo Grafford

All rights reserved.

No part of this book may be reproduced in any form without written permission from the author or publisher, except as permitted by U.S. copyright law.

ISBN: 978-1-63907-072-5

CONTENTS

Chapter 1: Here for You	1
Chapter 2: Spilling Secrets	18
Chapter 3: Pickup Riders	32
Chapter 4: Too Little, Too Late	48
Chapter 5: What Could've Been	64
Chapter 6: What Is	81
Chapter 7: Disappearing Act	100
Chapter 8: Fireworks	119
Chapter 9: Aftershocks	139
Chapter 10: Out with the Old, in with the New	157
Epilogue	174
Sneak Preview: Cowboy Accidentally Hitched for Christmas	188
Author's Note to the Reader	190
About the Author	193
Acknowledgments	195
Jo's Titles	197

CHAPTER 1: HERE FOR YOU

February

Ames Carson drummed his fingers on the checkout counter of Pinetop's most popular coffee bistro, wondering why it was taking so long to pour two simple cups of coffee. Unless, of course, the barista had run outside to grow and harvest the coffee beans first.

With a huff of impatience, he leaned farther over the counter, trying to figure out exactly what was happening inside the order preparation area at the Gingerbread House. The place was forever hopping with business — morning, noon, and night. But he'd been waiting a good ten minutes already.

And ten minutes felt like an eternity when a guy had a rented sleigh and a paid driver waiting outside.

If his spur-of-the-moment coffee stop took much longer, he'd be running late to his "not a date" with his "just a friend," Laura Lee, which would kind of defeat the whole purpose of their outing. He'd been trying without success for months to nudge their friendship toward something more. Inviting her on a Friday evening sleigh ride was his first attempt at a big gesture. According to the movies, girls liked big gestures. She'd said yes, so he was in the process of jumping the next big hurdle — gathering the perfect refreshments.

After breaking up with her fiancé a little over a year ago, Laura was still piecing her trampled heart back together. She deserved an evening that said *you come first with me*. An evening custom designed to pamper her with all of her favorite things. An evening that said *I'm gonna be here for you, no matter what*.

Ames fully intended to be the guy who ultimately convinced her to give love a second chance. That is, assuming the barista in front of him finished brewing their order before his two-hour sleigh ride reservation ended.

As she fiddled with countless knobs on a complicated-looking beverage machine, she shot a laughing glance over her shoulder. "Rela-a-ax. I'm almost finished." She looked college age, not that there were any colleges located in the tiny tourist town.

"Sorry." He shifted from one cowboy boot to the next. "It's just taking longer than I expected." A *lot* longer. He'd ordered coffee, for pity's sake, not a five-course meal.

"For two espressos with a shot of frothy hot cream that looks like it snowed on top?" The look the barista tossed his way had a little less warmth than before. Her dark ponytail was tied back in one of those food safety nets, so it slid forward against her shoulder like a fat beaver tail as she continued to work.

Ames nodded awkwardly. "Yeah, that sounds like what she wants." He'd written down word for word what Laura's younger sister, Lucy, had colorfully described as Laura's favorite beverage on the planet.

"When was the last time you steamed milk?" The young barista twirled his way, holding a silver wand over a small silver pitcher. The handle was pinched between her thumb and forefinger. A motor whirred and steam rose as she held the wand.

"Uh...never, I guess." How hard could it be to boil milk, though? He wondered if she'd dashed from the room when he wasn't looking to milk a cow in addition to growing the coffee beans.

She gave a snort of derision as she meticulously poured the bubbling white froth into the two cardboard cups in front of her. Though it was well past Christmas, the cups were still embossed with a holiday theme — a pale blue background shimmering with metallic white and silver snowflakes. The Gingerbread House logo was emblazoned in silver letters across the lids she snapped on the cups.

With a tight smile, she slid them across the counter to Ames. "Here you go. Two espressos mixed as fast as humanly possible."

"Thanks." To apologize for his impatience, he dropped a twenty-dollar bill on the counter before lifting the cups. One of the lids immediately popped off. "Uh-oh!" He abruptly set the cups back on the counter. It was a delicate balancing act to keep from sloshing the hot coffee over the rim.

The barista, who was in the act of eagerly reaching for the tip, paused in consternation to watch him wrestle with the lid. No matter how hard he tried, he was unable to get it snapped back on.

"Let me try." In a tone one might use with a toddler, she proceeded to take over his wrestling match with the lid. It proved to be a stubborn lid. She finally gave a sigh of defeat and tossed it in the trashcan.

"Think we got a defective lid." With a dramatic eye roll,

she pulled a fresh one off a nearby stack and expertly popped it into place. Her relief was palpable as she slid the espressos back in his direction. "First lid replacement is always on the house."

The *first* one? "Thanks." He really hoped she was joking, because he needed these lids to last through a couple-hour sleigh ride.

"Merry Friday and happy almost weekend," she trilled after him as he moved toward the rear exit.

He nodded instead of answering. By now, he should've been accustomed to all the creative holiday greetings floating around Pinetop, but he wasn't. Though he was currently living three-quarters of the year in a town that celebrated the holidays year round, he remained a firm believer that Christmas trees and mistletoe were for December. Not January, February, or March through November.

It was kind of ironic that he was putting so much effort into landing a date with a woman who wore an elf costume to work each day.

He used his shoulder to push open the door and stepped outside with a coffee cup fisted in each hand. His sleigh driver, Flash Billings, glanced up from his team of draft horses as he tromped back to the bright red sleigh waiting on the snowy strip behind the building. Mr. Billings was the town postmaster by day and tour guide by night.

"'Bout time you showed back up. Almost sent in a search party after you." The twinkle in his eyes brightened his grizzled appearance. Though he was often hired to dress as Santa for the holiday events around town, he looked more like Rumpelstiltskin when he was out of costume. He didn't have an extra ounce on his wiry frame, and his white beard was more of a long drizzle. It hung nearly to the waist of his insulated denim coat. His cheeks and nose were every bit as red as Santa's, though, making Ames feel guilty for making the older fella wait so long in the winter breeze.

"Hey, I'm really sorry about the wait. Here. Take one of these." On impulse, he held out one of the freshly made espressos.

"No, siree!" Mr. Billings gave a vehement head shake. "Appreciate the offer, but I've got my own brew to keep me warm — made just the I way like it." He gave another energetic head shake. "Black with no frills."

Black was how Ames preferred his coffee, too, but he was open to trying new things — especially things that might stand a chance of impressing Laura Lee. He climbed into the sleigh, tickled to pieces about the fresh blanket of snow that had fallen last night. Until he'd rolled out of bed this morning, he wasn't sure there'd be enough accumulation for a sleigh ride today. Now that they were in the second week of February, the end of winter was looming.

The slopes and ridges behind Main Street, however, were filled with more than enough snow for the sleigh runners to glide over. A few kids were lugging sleds up one of the hills. Their parents probably owned or rented one of the shops nearby.

A bustling, thriving tourist trap tucked into the side of a mountain, Pinetop was chock full of gift boutiques. Across Arizona, they were known as *the place* to do one's holiday shopping. On just about any given day, they had more visitors than permanent residents browsing through their stores. On snow days, most of the roads leading to bigger towns were closed until Pinetop's tiny road crew could safely clear the way. Today was probably one of those days, which meant the streets and sidewalks would be jammed with traffic all evening.

Going for a sleigh ride was the perfect way for Ames to avoid the crowds and have Laura all to himself for a couple of hours. Since he was in the presence of a fellow black coffee enthusiast at the moment, he didn't mind grumbling a little about the Gingerbread House behind their back.

"Apparently, those froo-froo drinks they make on the strip take half a century to brew." He grimaced at the memory of getting schooled on how to properly froth hot milk. "I was worried I might be stuck there the rest of the night and miss our sleigh ride altogether."

Mr. Billings guffawed. "Didn't have you pegged as a froo-froo kinda cowboy."

"Far from it, sir. I normally take my coffee black, same as you. The froo-froo stuff is for my friend, Laura." Ames settled back against the pair of quilts Mr. Billings had tossed into the sleigh. There was another side bench across from the one he was sitting on. His goal was to use only one of them this evening.

"Your friend, eh?" Flash Billings swiveled his head around just long enough to wink at him. "I was wondering if this was your first date or something."

"Or something." Ames glanced across the snowy terrain. "She's been through a lot. Not sure when she'll be ready to date again." He would continue to make it very clear to her this evening that he was available to fill that vacancy the moment she reached that point.

"So I've heard." Mr. Billings gave him a speculative look from his peripheral vision. "If it comes down to a fight, my money's on you, you loco bronc rider. I was as sorry as I could be to find out her ex had arrived in town this morning. Her parents aren't sure what he's got up his sleeve this time."

Ames' jaw dropped. For the second time in the space of a few minutes, he nearly spilled the coffee he was clutching in each gloved hand. "Did you say her ex is in town?" *Since when?* He cleared his throat, hoping he'd heard wrong even though he was pretty sure he hadn't. Though his exact age was a bit of a mystery, Flash Billings was probably the oldest citizen in town. A guy who knew everything there was to know about everybody around him.

"Yup. Sorry for being the bearer of bad news. Figured you already knew." The aging postmaster's voice waxed sympathetic as he guided his team of horses around a copse of evergreens.

"Nope." Ames angrily popped the P at the end of the word. His mind raced over all the possibilities of why Laura hadn't told him. Was she happy to see her ex? Was she still hopeful of picking up where they'd left off?

Ames didn't have all the details about their breakup. All he really knew was that her fiancé had broken things off only days before their wedding was supposed to have taken place.

"Believe me, his sudden appearance in town caught Laura's parents off guard, too." Flash Billings shook his head. "Ol' Haruki Lee wasn't sure how to break the news to her that Brex Morrison," his voice turned mocking, "the last of the gypsies, had decided to grace our small town with his presence." He raised a gloved hand to put air quotes around the words, *the last of the gypsies*.

Ames snorted. "The last of the who-sy what-ies?"

Mr. Billings shrugged. "Your guess is as good as mine. All I can tell you is that's what the fella wrote on his vendor application for the Sweetheart Spectacular. Who knows? Maybe this whole gypsy business means more to the Lees than it does to the rest of us."

A gypsy? It sounded like something out of a storybook to Ames. *Color me not impressed.* He didn't care what the guy called himself. It didn't change the fact that he was a spineless commitment-phobe, who'd broken the heart of a genuinely kind and decent woman.

He sat forward on the bench, resting his forearms on his knees in an attempt to keep the two espresso cups level. "So, that's his excuse for showing his face around here, eh?" Signing up as a craft fair vendor felt like the guy was grasping at straws. Was there any significance to the fact that he'd chosen to participate in Pinetop's annual Valentine themed fair? There were hundreds, maybe thousands, of other craft fairs around the country he could've chosen to participate in.

He shot a curious look at Flash Billings' gaunt shoulder blades. "What's he peddling, if you don't mind me asking?"

"Hand-crafted wooden toys." The postmaster's voice was grim.

"No kidding?" Ames tasted disgust. Apparently, that was something else Laura's ex had in common with her and her family. He was a blasted toy maker.

Technically, the Lees were certified furniture specialists. However, they'd made a name for themselves as the Merry Woodmakers, producing heirloom-quality Christmas toys. They'd got their start in an RV, roving from craft fair to craft fair across the country. A year ago, however, their fortune had changed after negotiating a contract to design toys exclusively for Santa's Toy Factory on Main Street. For the first time in years, they had a permanent address. They'd even purchased one of the chalets dotting the side of the mountain.

The last thing Laura Lee needed right now was some blast from her past skidding into town and yanking up the roots she was trying so hard to put down — certainly not some rolling stone who claimed to be the last of the gypsies. What did that even mean?

You'll have to go through me to get to her, buddy. Only when the coffee lid popped off the cup in his right hand did Ames realize how hard he'd been squeezing the cups. He spent the remaining few minutes of the drive to the Lees' home trying to clamp the loose lid back into place without spilling the espresso. His efforts proved futile.

Man! Two defunct coffee lids and the unexpected appearance of Laura's ex-fiancé were a rough start to the perfect evening he'd planned to treat her to.

I can still salvage this. He mentally braced himself as Flash Billings pulled across the front lawn of the Lee family's three-story chalet. It was a lovely cedar home overlooking the heart of Pinetop. Its snow-drenched roof made it look every bit a part of the postcard town sprawled below it.

Bronc riders are no sissies. I've got this!

Though Ames was no master toy maker like Brex Morrison apparently was, he was far from a nobody. He and his two brothers had spent most of their adult lives risking life and limb to make a name for themselves as rodeo champs. They had drawers full of buckles to prove it.

Ever since his oldest brother lost his lower right arm in a highway accident, however, the Carson brothers had been working hard to make a new name for themselves as indoor rodeo performers. The one-of-a-kind acting job was what had brought them to the festive mountain town and kept them there for the better part of a year.

Ames didn't know how long they'd remain there. Show ratings could be a fickle thing. However, there was one thing he was very sure about. He was desperate to know what it felt like to kiss Laura Lee before he returned to Dallas. If she didn't feel the same way about him, he'd soon be long gone. If she did return his feelings though...

He shook his head at the direction of his thoughts, struggling not to spill the espresso sloshing around in the dented, capless coffee cup. As soon as Mr. Billings brought his horses to a standstill, Ames bent to set the two cups of coffee on the floorboard. Then he gingerly stepped out of the sleigh, trying not to rock it too much in the process.

"Thanks!" He moved to the driver's side of the sleigh to catch the postman's eye. "I'll be right back with Laura." Jogging up the snowy sidewalk to the front porch, he was a little surprised to discover that no one had cleared the walkway. Normally, Mr. Lee was fastidious about details like that. Though the sun was dipping on the horizon, there was no porch light on, either.

Hoping everything was okay, he used the toe of his boot to clear a path up the short flight of stairs that would make it all the easier to escort Laura back down them. Before he could tap the doorbell button, the porch light flickered on. The front door popped open.

"Hey!" Laura stepped outside and pulled the door shut behind her. "You made it!" Though she had her face averted, it was impossible to miss the fact that her eyelids were puffy from crying.

Since it wasn't in Ames' DNA to play games, he stepped directly in her path and reached for her shoulders. "What's wrong?" Though he suspected her ex was what was wrong, he preferred to hear it from the horse's mouth.

Despite the shadows beneath her eyes, she looked amazing in a white puff jacket with a matching beanie and mittens. Her wavy hair tumbled past her shoulders like a dark waterfall. To him, she was the most beautiful woman in the country, splotchy cheeks and all. That was how bad he had it for her.

She gave a damp sniffle. "Can we please not talk about it right now? I just..." She glanced around his shoulder. "I just want to enjoy our sleigh ride, okay?"

"Okay." Unable to resist the urge to comfort her, he tugged her closer for a quick, reassuring hug. When he lowered his arms, she gave a squeak of pain.

Her head jerked back a little, making him realize that the little plastic hook on his gloves had gotten caught in her hair. It was the hook that clasped his gloves together when he wasn't wearing them.

"I'm sorry." He fumbled with the hook and managed to

make her wince again. Gritting his teeth, he had to remove his other glove with his teeth to bare his fingers. Only then did he achieve the dexterity required to release the silky strand of hair that had become snagged.

Her eyes were shimmering with a fresh round of unshed tears by the time he finished. "Listen, I'm really sorry," he muttered again, hating himself a little for being so clumsy.

"It's okay." She smiled through the mist at him. "No good deed goes unpunished, huh?" In a playful attempt to help him put his glove back on, she leaned his way at the same time he bent his head to accomplish the same task.

Their foreheads collided.

Her gasp went straight to his heart, nearly strangling it. "I'm such an idiot," he groaned.

"No, you're not!" She tugged his glove the rest of the way on while he was still blinking away stars. "You're my best friend in the universe."

Ouch! Ames wasn't sure if the sharp pain shooting through his skull was from bumping noggins or from being slammed solidly back into the friend zone. However, tonight wasn't about him, his needs, or his wants. It was about serving up the kind of evening Laura deserved. He wanted to pamper and spoil her in ways that no one else had ever done. He wanted to show her what it was like to be with a guy who truly cared about her. He wanted tonight to be a night she'd never forget.

It was certainly shaping up to be unforgettable, just not in the way he'd hoped. At this very moment, he'd gladly settle for one thing going right. Just one thing!

As she moved down the porch stairs ahead of him, her left hand shot toward the railing. "Oh!" Her gasp filled his ears as her snow boots scissored out from beneath her.

He lunged her way and reached for her elbow to steady her. In the process, his left boot shot out from beneath him on the slick stairs. His taller, broader frame catapulted toward hers, threatening to crush her.

It was all he could do to skid his long legs beneath hers in order to absorb the brunt of their tumble. He grunted in discomfort as her weight slipped and slid against him, jamming him more fully into the hard edge of the stairs.

"Oh, my goodness! Are you okay?" Laura slithered like a wet eel against him to twist around and crane anxiously up at him.

He'd probably have bruises the size of San Antonio on his shoulders and backside tomorrow, but he managed to give her an affirmative nod.

"Liar!" She spat out the word, struggling to her feet and reaching for him with both hands.

Since he'd already established the fact that he was an idiot, he accepted her help and tried not to groan too loudly as she helped pull him upright. He took a tentative step to make sure nothing was broken. "Please assure me you're alright."

"I'm, er…" She leaned into him, pressing her face to his chest. Her shoulders started to shake.

"Laura, darling!" He gathered her close, careful to keep his arms snaked around her waist to avoid snagging her hair again. "Talk to me."

A muffled sound erupted from her, then another one. That's when he realized she was laughing, not crying.

His shoulders slumped in relief. "Man! You had me going there for a sec." He spoke against the top of her head, enjoying her flowery scent and nearness. Though he'd come close to breaking a few bones in the process, having her in his arms like this was worth every bruise rising on his body.

"Thank you." She slid from his embrace and took a shaky step back.

"For what?" He met her gaze ruefully. "Nearly yanking your hair out by the roots or almost breaking your neck?"

"None of the above, you dork." She punched him lightly in the chest. "Thanks for making me laugh. I needed that." By some miracle, her tears had vanished, and the splotchiness staining her cheeks was fast fading.

He caught her hand and used it to tow her the rest of the way down the sidewalk toward the sleigh. He didn't dare meet Flash Billings' gaze, not wanting to know what the old fellow was thinking. Ames was all too aware that the beginning of his perfectly planned evening was a complete disaster. He wasn't sure there was any coming back from their tumble down the porch stairs.

He was extra careful as he assisted Laura into the sleigh and extra gentle as he lifted and tucked one of the quilts snuggly around her waist.

"Careful!" She pointed down in alarm, but it was too late.

The lower edge of the quilt caught the side of the coffee cup on the right. It toppled over, sending rivulets of frothy brown coffee across the floorboard of the sleigh.

Ames dove forward to save the second cup, grateful that at least one of the espressos had survived his hapless fling of the quilt. "It looks like your cup is the sole survivor of my clumsiness."

He couldn't have been more wrong. As he started to hand it to her, the breeze whipped off the lid and sent it flying over the edge of the sleigh. "What in the—?" He stared after it in puzzlement, realizing he must've knocked over the good cup, which meant the one in his hand was the one he'd popped the lid loose on earlier.

Laura's startled gasp alerted him to the fact that he was tipping the cup. Steaming coffee sloshed onto the quilt covering her lap. A dark, damp spot spread across the fabric.

The sleigh passed over a bumpy part of the yard, sending a second splash of coffee over the rim.

Laura abruptly removed the cup from Ames' hand and tossed it over the side of the sleigh. "This is clearly not my night." She wrinkled her nose at him. "It's me, not you. Trust me. I should've never left home this evening. I've been a wreck ever since I found out..." She bit her lip to silence the rest of what she'd been about to say.

Ames gusted out a breath, pretty sure he knew what was bothering her. "Ever since you found out Brex Morrison was in town, eh?" No matter how much she didn't want to talk about him, there was no point in continuing to beat around the bush. Her ex was the proverbial elephant perched on the bench between them.

"Yes," she sighed. "Wait!" She tipped her face up to his, looking distressed. "How did you—?"

"It's a small town," he reminded, flinging the soggy quilt into the damp floorboard. He'd offer to have it dry cleaned. At the sight of the damp spot on the thighs of Laura's jeans, he unzipped his leather coat and started to shrug out of it.

"Don't you dare!" Her voice grew so threatening that he stopped.

When she shivered, his hands started moving again. "I'm not gonna let you freeze," he protested.

"Right back atcha, cowboy!" She leaned forward to snatch the other quilt off the bench across from them. "You planned an amazing evening for us. There's no way I'm going to thank you by allowing you to turn into a block of ice." She tossed the quilt over both of them, tucking it carefully around him the way he'd tucked the other quilt around her only minutes earlier. She was shivering like crazy by the time she finished.

Ames drew her snugly against his side, sharing as much of his body heat as he could. Then he called to Flash Billings, "You'd best turn around and get us back to her place pronto.

She's soaked to the skin from all the coffee I spilled on her." It was no wonder he was still a single guy. Rough and tough bronc riders like him simply weren't made of boyfriend material.

The aging postmaster obligingly drove his team of horses in a wide circle and retraced their path. In short order, he had them back in front of the Lees' chalet.

"Sorry about tonight." Ames gave Laura one last lingering hug before letting her go. "This was far from the evening I had planned for us."

"I know." Despite her own misery, Laura's voice was filled to the brim with empathy for him. It was just how kindhearted of a person she was. "Come inside," she urged, tugging on his hand. "We can thaw out together over a fresh cup of coffee. My treat this time."

"Nah, that's okay." He curled his upper lip at her, anxious to put an end to the nightmarish evening. "You're the one who—" A violent shiver came out of nowhere, interrupting his sentence.

She snickered. "I'm pretty sure you're wearing as much coffee as I am, cowboy." Her teeth chattered over the last few words.

She threw off the quilt and hopped out of the sleigh.

Ames gave Flash Billings an apologetic look. "Listen, I intend to cover the dry cleaning bill for those quilts."

"That won't be necessary, son." His tone was far more cheerful than the dismal situation warranted. "I'll throw 'em in the washer like I always do, and they'll be right as rain by the time you reschedule your sleigh ride. You've got at least an hour and a half left of the slot you reserved."

"Thank you, sir. I'll, um...take a look at your schedule." Ames highly doubted he'd be rescheduling. What woman in her right mind would want to relive an evening like this one?

He stepped from the sleigh and hurried after Laura,

keeping a careful grip on the railing as they made their way back up the stairs they'd fallen down earlier.

Moments later, they stood inside the entry foyer, facing each other. The interior of the chalet was surprisingly silent, telling him they were alone.

Though it was much warmer inside, Laura gave another shiver. Then she flung herself into his arms. "Thank you, Ames. For the sleigh ride and the coffee." She gave a chuckle that held a hint of a sob around the edges. "Lucy let it slip that you asked her for my favorite coffee order, so I know you put a lot of effort into this evening."

He hugged her back. "Much good it did me." He was the proverbial bull in a china shop. *Can't seem to do anything right where you're concerned.* "Where's Lucy, by the way?"

"Out with friends." She snuggled closer to him.

"What about your parents?" It seemed awfully late on a Friday night for them not to be home from work already.

"It's their anniversary weekend," she explained in a muffled voice against his shirt, "so Dad reserved one of the airbnb rooms above the toy store."

Guess that explains the snowy sidewalk outside. Ames grunted and pressed his cheek to the top of her head. "I'm going to go out on a limb and predict he's probably not busy spilling coffee all over your mother as we speak."

"Just stop it already!" Laura chuckled again. "You're being way too hard on yourself. In case I've never told you this, you are — hands down — the nicest guy I've ever met."

"Nice," he grumbled. "Yay." *Not.* Nice was most definitely *not* the kind of evening he'd been gunning for. More like spectacular.

"You are," she protested, leaning back in his embrace to meet his gaze. "Nobody has ever gone to that kind of effort on my behalf. For reals. You're always doing stuff for me, and it means the world to me, okay? Spilled coffee and all."

"Really?" Though it was far from a romantic moment, standing there in the foyer shivering together, his gaze dipped to her rosy lips. Someday he was going to steal that kiss he'd been dreaming about day and night for months.

Not now, though. She wasn't ready.

"Really." She gently wiggled out of his embrace and reached for his hands, towing him backward toward the kitchen. "Now let's go make some more of that espresso that didn't survive the sleigh ride."

CHAPTER 2: SPILLING SECRETS

As Laura pulled Ames toward the kitchen, it dawned on her that his expression had changed. He still had the usual swagger in his step, and his blond eyebrows were still raised in the usual cocky quirk beneath the brim of his Stetson, but his eyelids had grown distinctively heavier.

Unless her overwrought emotions were causing her to misread the situation, his attention also seemed a little fixated on her mouth all of a sudden. A little *too* fixated for a guy who was supposed to be nothing more than a friend.

He wants to kiss me. The realization sank into her dazed thoughts, bringing a level of awareness between them she'd never experienced before. The air practically vibrated with it.

Ames Smoking Hot Carson actually wants to kiss me! The tall, windblown, sun-kissed cowboy who — along with his two brothers — had quickly become the biggest heartthrobs in Pinetop. Not only were all three of them champion bronc riders, he'd additionally found the time to earn his pilot's license. He was the real deal, the whole package — the very hunky, very single version of it.

Though Laura continued walking backwards in front of

him, she abruptly dropped his hands. It was as if they'd turned into two fistfuls of burning lava or something.

"What's wrong?" He stalked playfully after her on legs that were slightly bowed from a lifetime in the saddle. "You allergic to me all of a sudden?"

"I..." She shook her head, at a momentary loss for words as the truth continued to splash through her. How had she missed what had been happening right beneath her nose for months?

All his running ahead of her to open doors, all of his offers to carry her store purchases, all of his last-minute offers to drive her home from work where he so conveniently happened to show up at just the right time nearly every evening... And don't even get her started on tonight's fiasco in the sleigh. It had been his first attempt at setting the stage for an actual date with her. She was sure of it.

Her shoulder grazed the doorway of the kitchen on her way through it, making her stumble.

Ames was there, like he always was, reaching for her upper arms to steady her while gazing down at her with that half-questioning, sort of hopeless look he gave her sometimes.

"Ames," she breathed, squeezing her eyelids shut to give herself a moment to catch her breath. "I didn't know," she whispered shakily. "Not until tonight. Not until...just now." She still wasn't sure how she'd missed it. Maybe that part of her was so damaged that it wasn't working right anymore.

"Yeah, well, now you do," he growled, dropping his hands from her arms. There was no hesitation in his answer. No sheepishness or shame. Maybe a little anger, but it was directed at himself, not her. He was way too honest to dodge or deny her discovery that he cared more for her than a friend should.

Her eyelids fluttered open. "Were you ever going to tell me?"

"Yep."

"When?" Thankfully, the door frame was still within reaching distance. She rested a hand against it for support.

"I don't know, Laura." He raised and lowered his shoulders, looking perplexed. "When you were ready, I guess. I wanted to be friends first. To get to know you better and give you a chance to get to know me better."

"That's really sweet of you." Her words didn't do his actions justice. He'd been so much more than sweet. He'd been empathetic and understanding. He'd been patient and kind. He'd put her needs before his own. Though he was normally a leap first and think afterward kind of guy, at least when it came to his rodeo stunts, he'd done a whole lot more thinking first than acting when it came to her. It spoke volumes about his character. It also told her he meant business.

About her. About them.

He pushed his hat back a little. "Sweet certainly isn't an adjective my brothers would use to describe me. They'd laugh their rear ends off if they heard you call me that."

"Then I won't say it in front of them." She blushed as soon as the words left her. *Could I have said anything stupider?* Giving herself a mental shake, she let go of the door frame and straightened.

Or tried to.

Ames stepped closer. "You can call me anything you want, Laura. Any time. Any place. I can handle the fallout with my brothers."

"You *are* sweet," she pointed out shyly, tipping her head back against the wood trim. "Maybe not to them." She gave a nervous chuckle. "But you are to me. You always have been." It made her a little sad that she'd been so stuck in recovery mode from her breakup with Brex that she'd failed to see that before now. Another thought struck her, making her eyes widen in horror. "Is it because you feel sorry for me?"

His eyebrows rose in astonishment. "Is that what you really think?"

She shook her head uncertainly. "Honestly, Ames? I don't know what to think anymore. It's been so long since I've been in good head space. Broken engagements can do that to a person, I guess."

A fierce expression flashed across his angular features, making her insides tremble. "I reckon it doesn't help that your ex is back in town."

"No." She was unable to quell a shiver. "It doesn't."

He immediately shrugged out of his leather jacket. This time, she didn't try to stop him. "Here." He draped it around her shoulders, smoothing his large hands down the sleeves to mold it more snugly against her arms. "Better?"

"Yes." The truth was, her whole world had taken a turn for the better the moment he'd stepped into it. They'd known each other for the better part of a year now. He was the biggest reason her heart was on the road to recovery.

"I'm still gonna be here for you, okay?" He held her gaze steadily. "Ex or no ex in the mix, I plan to keep being your person, Laura." He drew a heavy breath. "As long as you'll let me."

"You mean you'll keep being my friend?" Her voice rose to such a high note that she hardly recognized it as her own.

"Always." His voice was low and tender. Like before, there was no hesitation in his answer.

"That's it?" she pressed threadily.

"I didn't say that." His blue gaze burned into hers, allowing her a glimpse of what he was leaving unsaid.

She caught her lower lip between her teeth. "Then what, Ames? I've never been good at guessing games."

His gaze dipped to her mouth again. "I want to be here for you the way you deserve. I want to be your most faithful listener when you need to talk. Your biggest cheerleader for all the new and innovative stuff you keep testing out at work. I want to be your go-to guy during the good times and the bad times."

She had to remind herself to breathe. If she was being perfectly honest with herself, he'd already been serving in every single one of those roles. She just hadn't thought about it that way before now.

"And eventually," his voice dropped to a lower, huskier note, "I want to steal a kiss from you, preferably before the Carson brothers leave town for good."

Her lips parted in alarm. "You're leaving?" Apprehension flooded her. "When?"

He shrugged. "No exact date, but we're not going to be in Pinetop forever. We've already been here months longer than we originally planned."

She nodded sadly, knowing he was referring to the double extension the owners at Castellano's had already made to the Carson brothers' contract to perform at their indoor rodeo.

He ducked his head a little to study her expression. "You gonna miss me when I'm gone?"

"Very much." She glanced away from him, no longer able to endure the intensity of his gaze. "Do you, um, mind if I get started on that coffee I promised you?" She blindly turned away from him and finished stepping into the kitchen.

"Nope. You want some help?" She heard the footfalls of his boots against the tile floor as he followed her.

She smiled despite her sadness. "Are you telling me you actually know how to make a shot of espresso?" His sudden interest in espresso was surprising, considering his much simpler taste in black.

"Does watching the barista do it earlier count?"

She tossed a knowing look at him as she made her way to the fridge. "If you're referring to standing at the counter and tapping the toe of your boot impatiently? No."

He snorted. "You know me so well."

Apparently, not well enough to notice you were falling for me. Guilt spurted through her midsection, throwing her emotionally off balance again. "I thought I knew you," she confessed softly as she pulled open the stainless steel fridge door and withdrew a carton of milk.

"You still know me." He sounded matter-of-fact. "I'm the same guy I've always been. My feelings for you haven't changed from the get go."

"What I know about your feelings has changed, though," she reminded quietly. "It's a lot to wrap my brain around, Ames." She still wasn't sure what she thought about having her closest friend crushing on her. For one thing, the timing was off. Her heart was already twisted into enough emotional knots, and here he was tying another one into the mix. It was almost too much!

"Take all the time you need. I'm in no hurry." He leaned back against the kitchen counter and folded his arms, watching her as she went to work measuring out coffee grounds.

Is that so? She flicked an irritated look his way. "Says the guy who just finished informing me that he won't be in town forever." Pulling open the overhead cabinet, she withdrew a clean white mug and slid it beneath the coffee dispenser spigot. Then she pushed the brew button.

She could feel his gaze on her as she left the kitchen and hurried across the great room to start a fire. She shed both of their jackets, tossing them on the sofa on her way to the fireplace. Though the central heat was blowing through the vents, there was just something about an honest-to-goodness real fire that never failed to warm her all the way to her toes.

"Maybe it's for the best," he called across the great room to her. "Think about it, Laura. If you decide you don't like having a best friend who has more than friendly feelings for you, then I'll be out of your hair soon."

"Please don't say that." She blinked rapidly as she dragged her feet back to the kitchen. She was only two blinks away from breaking down again. "I already said I'm going to miss you." She couldn't bear the thought of him no longer living next door. No longer meeting her after work. No longer bumbling his way through all the crazy, wonderful things he was forever doing for her.

"Maybe it's just the dumb bronc rider in me talking, but I'm going to take that as a compliment." He sounded inordinately pleased with himself.

She wrinkled her nose at him, not caring for the way he'd put himself down. "I've called you a lot of things inside my head, Ames Carson, but not once have I ever used the word dumb." She realized her mistake the moment his gaze sharpened.

"Do tell, Miss Lee. What exactly have you been calling me inside your head?" He leaned teasingly closer to her as she measured out the milk and started frothing it. "This I've gotta hear."

"Cocky," she snapped without looking up. "Only a very cocky cowboy would want me to elaborate on something like that."

"Cocky," he repeated, sounding amused. "I've certainly been called worse."

"Not by me you haven't, and you never will." She chose her next words carefully, not wanting to hurt his feelings any worse than she probably already had. "I care too much for you."

"But," he sighed, straightening again. "I hear a very loud but coming."

"I may not care for you the same way you care for me...or the way you want me to..." His wry expression told her that she was doing a very bad job of explaining herself. "But I do care for you. A lot. Which is why I'm going to be brutally honest with you about something." She all but shoved the mug of espresso at him that she'd just finished brewing.

"We're friends, remember?" He accepted the mug with a mocking look. "No need to be brutal."

She rolled her eyes at him. Already knowing he wasn't going to like the espresso, she didn't bother mixing a second one for herself. Instead, she placed a clean mug under the spigot and started brewing a cup of plain black coffee.

He took an extra noisy sip just to be silly, then made a sound of disgust. "Flash Billings was right. I'm most definitely *not* a froo-froo kind of guy when it comes to coffee."

"I know." She watched the cup of plain black coffee finish filling. "That's why what you did for me tonight was so incredibly special." She lifted the steaming black brew and handed it to him. "Here. Let's trade."

Their fingers brushed during the hand off. Though they'd touched many times in the past — everything from bear hugs to playful punches — this time was different. Tiny aftershocks of awareness prickled across her hand and tingled all the way to her heart.

"It's got my cooties on it." He winked at her.

"Thanks for the warning." She deliberately turned the mug around and sipped from the same spot he had. "Will you look at that? I'm still standing."

He crooked a smile at her. "I hope it doesn't bother you to hear me say that was hot. Way hot!"

A breathy chuckle spilled out of her. "I honestly have no idea what to think about this new version of you."

He waggled his eyebrows at her. "It's not new."

She beckoned him to follow her to the pair of stools

scooted up to the bar behind them. A large square was cut into the wall to create a pass-through cubby from the kitchen to the vaulted dining area on the other side. It bled seamlessly into the great room beyond it.

Ever the perfect gentleman, he held out her stool for her. Only after they were seated and cradling their respective cups of coffee did she sigh, "Okay. Here's the not so brutal truth." Without warning, tears welled in her eyes and trickled warmly down her cheeks.

"Whoa!" Ames set his coffee mug down with a clatter of porcelain against granite. He spun his stool toward her and reached for her hands. "Look at me, Laura."

She miserably met his gaze, hating the fact that he was seeing her like this.

"You can tell me anything, just like you've been doing the whole time we've known each other."

She shook her head, feeling close to melting down into a full ugly cry. "I don't want to hurt your feelings."

"I'm a bronc rider, Laura." His voice was dry. "We're not exactly made of glass."

"You can be hurt," she quavered, "and I don't want to be the one to do it."

"Then hurry up and lay it on me." His expression was unreadable. "The quicker you rip off the Band-Aid, the less it'll sting."

She swallowed hard. "Don't say I didn't warn you."

"I won't," he assured her in such a gentle voice that her tears flowed all the faster. He laced his fingers through hers.

"Right up until this evening when I finally realized you, um..." She gulped.

His eyes glinted wickedly at her. "When it became crystal clear just how badly I want to kiss you, eh?"

She blushed. "Yes. That." *So not helping.* "I'd been trying to picture what it would look like if Brex and I actually got back together."

He looked stunned, and not in a good way. "Come again?"

"I know how bad that must sound to you." She shook her head, glancing away from him. "But that's what I've spent the past year imagining." She sniffled loudly. "Everyone in my family thinks he's an awful person for getting cold feet right before our wedding, but that doesn't change the fact that he's the guy I almost married. Right or wrong, Ames, I chose him once upon a time, and he chose me."

"Why, Laura?" Ames sounded abnormally calm. He was taking this so much better than she'd expected. "Why did you choose him?"

It was a good question. A fair one. "We had so much in common, I guess." She raised and lowered her shoulders. "We were both toy makers. We were both living on the road, traveling from craft fair to craft fair without any one place to call home. It was a different sort of life and not an easy one — always switching schools while growing up, always leaving our friends behind. It was nice to finally meet someone who truly got me."

Ames' expression remained hooded. "Was he your first kiss?"

"No." She chuckled damply at the memory. "The honors for that go to a kid named Billy." She sniffled again. "In case you're wondering, he and I met in kindergarten."

A grin spread across Ames' face. He let go of one of her hands to pull a napkin from the holder on the edge of the counter. Holding it out to her, he drawled, "Just sizing up the competition."

She used the napkin to dab her cheeks dry. "We moved, and I never saw him again." She seriously doubted she would even recognize the adult version of him.

"What about your first crush?" Ames prodded.

"Same kid."

"Alright." He reached for her hand again, damp napkin and all. "So I can't be your first crush, your first kiss, or your first fiancé. Triple bummer!" He tangled their fingers together. "Doesn't mean I can't be your last." He paused for a few heartbeats. "When you're ready, of course."

"Ames," Laura gasped, shaking her head at the helpless longing staining his features. "Haven't you heard a word I said?"

"Clearly, I have, because now I know what I'm up against."

"Please don't do this to yourself." She squeezed his fingers. "You deserve better than this, Ames. Better than me. I'm way too messed up right now, and I don't know when I'm going to get it all sorted out." *If ever.* She was both dreading and looking forward to seeing Brex Morrison again. To be fair, she was mostly dreading it. He'd texted to ask if they could meet up somewhere in town for breakfast in the morning. Her younger sister was going to pitch a fit when she found out Laura was actually considering his request. The way she saw it, Brex still owed her an explanation.

"I appreciate your honesty." Ames jutted his squared-off chin at her. "Now maybe you'll appreciate a little bit of the same from me." He used their joined hands to tug her closer. "I care about you, Laura. It's not some switch I can just turn off, no matter how inconvenient it is for you to have a guy like me around."

"Ames," she sighed, squirming a little on the stool and wishing he wasn't being quite so honest. "You're not an inconvenience, for pity's sake! I'm not sure why you're always putting yourself down like that."

"Maybe because I understand I'm the guy you didn't ask for in your life, but that's too bad. You've got me, anyway." He winked at her. "So unless you send me packing, I'm gonna be here for you, okay?"

"Ames, I'll say it again. That's not fair to you," she protested.

"It's my choice," he insisted.

"I should tell you no." It was the only right thing to do.

"But you won't," he taunted, arching an eyebrow at her. "Because there's a part of you that wants to know just as badly as I do where this is leading." He gave her a pointed look. "Between us."

She glanced down at their hands. "Since we're laying it all out there, there's something you should know. Brex is asking me to meet him for breakfast in the morning."

He winced. It was barely discernible, but there was no way to miss it since they were still holding hands. "What did you tell him?"

"I haven't texted him back yet," she admitted.

"Why not?"

"I don't know." It was hard to explain, even to herself. "Receiving his text felt like having an old wound ripped open. Regardless, he owes me a better explanation than the one he gave me when he broke things off between us."

"You're really giving me the warm fuzzies about this guy, darling."

Despite the seriousness of their conversation, she snickered. "Ooo, sarcastic *and* cocky." A delicious feeling had washed over her the second he'd called her darling, but she wasn't ready to acknowledge it in front of him. Or read too much into it yet. It was sweet, though. Really, really sweet.

"I'm on a roll." He reluctantly let go of her hands. "Let me know when and where you decide to meet Gypsy Boy, and I'll be sure to crowd into a booth somewhere in the room."

She made a face at him. "I'm not sure that's how this is supposed to work."

"Hey, all's fair in love and war." He lifted his coffee mug, guzzling down the rest of it. "At least, that's what everybody says." He set his mug down and stood. "Either way, my offer to have your back still stands. You want me there tomorrow, and I'll be there. End of story."

She stood, in no mood to finish her espresso that was fast cooling to room temperature. "I should probably see what Brex has to say. My gut says he's in town to see me. Avoiding him isn't going to make him leave any sooner."

Ames studied her thoughtfully, looking like he was weighing every word that came out of her. "How about the Peppermint Palace?" Though they were discussing her meeting someone besides him for breakfast tomorrow, he seemed in no hurry to end the conversation. He propped his hands loosely on his hips. "It's a public place. Big. Plenty of witnesses and plenty of places for your future boyfriend to keep a low profile in the background."

A warm feeling burned in the pit of the coldness that had been plaguing her insides all afternoon. It grew bigger and glowed brighter. "Despite every reasonable objection popping into my head right now, I want to say yes so badly that it hurts."

"Then there's your answer." He reached out to run the back of a finger down her jawline. "I'm gonna let you in on a little secret. One of the reasons us bronc riders survive out there is because we never go into the ring without an exit strategy. There's a couple of pickup riders keeping their eyeballs on us at all times, ready to come to our aid at a moment's notice and help get us out of harm's way. Why should tomorrow be any different?"

Why, indeed? It was the question of the century.

"The way I see it," he continued in a gravelly voice, "you've been hurt enough already. It's time for someone to show this gypsy fella how a real man would treat a woman like you."

Wo-o-ow! Her lips parted in amazement. Her favorite cocky, sarcastic cowboy was gone. In his place was her fiercely protective best friend, who was ready to prove to her that he was capable of becoming more. Much more.

"You deserve to be adored, Laura Lee." He brushed his finger down her jawline again. "Cherished. Spoiled. Made to feel every ounce as incredible as you are." He retraced the same outline with his finger. "I know you didn't get the best demonstration of what I'm talking about during our tumble down the stairs earlier." He grimaced at the memory. "Or the way we bumped heads, or the coffee I spilled on you afterward."

"Eight o'clock," she interrupted, finally making up her mind. "I'll tell him to meet me at the Peppermint Palace at eight o'clock sharp."

Ames dropped his hand. "Unless you tell me otherwise, your pickup rider will be present and accounted for." The glint in his gaze told her he was actually looking forward to it.

She could only hope she wasn't making the biggest mistake of her life by dragging someone as big-hearted and loyal as him into her personal mess.

CHAPTER 3: PICKUP RIDERS

"You're gonna do what?" Flint was so distracted by Ames' announcement that he momentarily lost focus during their arm wrestling match. They were seated at a tall square bar-height table that currently served as their dining room table.

Ames slammed his youngest brother's fist backwards against the rustic wood tabletop, ending the match. "I win!" He raised his fists in the air and gave them a shake of victory.

"Rematch," Flint howled. His glare indicated more loudly than words that he knew he hadn't been beaten fair and square.

Ames glanced at his watch. "No can do, bro. It's nearly midnight, and I have a breakfast date at the Peppermint Palace in the morning." The name of the restaurant was as froo-froo as the espresso Laura had brewed for him earlier.

Flint's glare became more pronounced. "Sounds to me like someone else besides you has that breakfast date with your favorite toy maker."

"Doesn't matter." Ames slapped the air, dismissing the claim. "I'm the one who's gonna have her back. Always have and always will." *So long as she lets me,* he added inside his head.

There was no way he was going to admit how terrified he was that Laura might allow her ex to talk her into kissing and making up. *You had your chance, Gypsy Boy, and you blew it.* But some of the nicest women in the world let the meanest guys continue to walk all over them. He sent up a silent prayer that Laura would prove stronger than that.

He knew before laying eyes on Brex Morrison that the guy must be a real piece of work to have so callously broken the heart of a woman as lovely as Laura. He didn't care what Brex's reasons were. Anyone dumb enough to walk away from her the way he had didn't deserve her, plain and simple.

Help me prove it to her, Lord. Help me be the guy who finally gets to adore and cherish her the way she deserves.

He considered it a good sign that Laura wanted him at the restaurant with her in the morning so she wouldn't have to face her ex alone. Yeah, he got that it wasn't a typical dating situation, having to witness her meeting up with another guy. However, an extraordinary woman like Laura was worth going to extraordinary efforts for in order to win her heart.

Flint shook his head in disgust. "I hate to break it to you, but there's no such thing as a pickup rider on a date. Despite how much I like Laura, I think she's using you, bro."

"Not true. I'm the one who offered to have her back." Ames raised his hands in defense of her. "This was my idea from start to finish. Not hers. I even suggested the venue."

Flint looked even more disgusted as he stood and pushed his stool back from the table. "Just give me one good reason why you're gonna put yourself out there for her like that." His expression indicated he didn't think anything good would come from it.

Ames spread his hands. "She's the one, Flint. That's my reason. My one and only reason."

"Man," Flint groaned, yanking off his Stetson and sending it flying like a frisbee onto their leather sofa in the living room. It was a good shot. His hat landed on the middle cushion and stayed. He swung back in his older brother's direction. "Are you sure about this? About her?"

Ames nodded. His youngest brother was rarely serious. On the few occasions when he was, Ames preferred to give him the bald-faced truth. "I've prayed about our relationship enough to know that she's the one for me."

"Even though she's dating another guy?" Flint still didn't look convinced. He unbuttoned his fleece plaid shirt and shrugged out of it, revealing a navy graphic t-shirt underneath.

Ames knew what it looked like, but he couldn't do anything about that. Not right this second, at any rate. "Pretty sure this is a onetime meet up, and I wouldn't call it a date."

"Are you listening to yourself?" Flint tipped his head back to emit a howl of supreme frustration at the ceiling.

"Trying not to," Ames admitted ruefully. "I get how it sounds to you, bro, but I'm too busy keeping the faith to dwell on the negative."

"I want to believe you. I do. But what if you're wrong?" Flint met his gaze again, looking like he was tasting something sour.

Ames spread his hands. "If that ends up being the case," and he would be praying hard that it wasn't, "I can return home to run Canyon Creek Ranch ahead of the rest of y'all. Permanently, if that's where I'm needed the most." The three of them had never intended to be away from Dallas for this long. Though they had a top-notch foreman helping oversee the day-to-day operations of their horse ranch, it wasn't the same as being directly involved. There was no substitute for hands-on management. If one of the brothers didn't return home soon, they might as well start discussing the pros and cons of selling the place.

Flint was silent for a moment. Then he shook his head dejectedly. "The lengths a guy will go to dodge an arm wrestling rematch."

Ames barked out a laugh, appreciating the note of levity Flint had managed to introduce into a conversation that was getting way too serious. "Whatever you have to tell yourself to make you feel better about losing tonight." Before his youngest brother could formulate a worthy comeback, he moved to the side of the living room to jog up the stairs. His bedroom was located on the second floor.

Whistling to drown out any further pithy commentary from below, he cut across his bedroom and headed straight for the shower. Peeling out of his coffee stained clothing, he stepped beneath the hot spray.

"Lord, depending on how things go in the morning, I may need You to step in as *my* Pickup Rider." Laura was right about him. Despite his scarred and callused hands and arms, his heart was far from bullet proof, especially where she was concerned.

He was already bracing himself for the possibility she might decide to reconcile with her ex in the morning, instead of showing him the road like he deserved. Despite the strong front Ames had attempted to put on in front of Flint, keeping the faith where Laura was concerned was turning out to be one of the toughest challenges he'd ever faced.

❋

AFTER STARING AT THE CEILING MOST OF THE NIGHT, AMES rolled out of bed and yanked on his jeans before his alarm went off. He'd checked online the evening before to verify the hours of operation for the Peppermint Palace. They opened at eight o'clock on the dot — right when Laura was scheduled to meet her ex there. Ames planned to be first in line and seated before they were. If she happened to catch sight of him getting served ahead of her, that was even better.

Flint was already nursing a cup of coffee when Ames strode into the kitchen. He was staring out the window over the sink with his elbows resting on the countertop.

Ames stifled a yawn. "I'm not awake enough for a rematch, if that's why you're here." He purposely bumped into Flint on his way to the coffee pot, making some of his coffee slosh over the rim of his cup into the sink.

"Now you owe me a cup of coffee and a rematch." Flint straightened and arched his back lazily to stretch it.

"It was one sip. Get over it." Ames reached for the pot Flint had brewed and helped himself to a brimming mug of it.

"Don't think I will," the punk drawled. "I let one rematch slide, and now you're pushing coffee boundaries. You're out of control, bro."

Ames stomped to the bar and hiked one hip up on a stool. "Do me a favor and hold the drama king routine until I've downed my first cup of joe. Better yet, save it until after I leave the house."

"I gotta better idea." Flint followed him to the bar and leaned forward on the counter, facing him. His hair was still tousled from sleep, and his plaid shirt wasn't yet buttoned over his undershirt.

"I seriously doubt it," Ames grumbled into his mug of coffee, trying to ignore him. Unfortunately, Flint was a force of nature that wasn't easy to ignore.

"Then you'd be wrong, because I'm coming with you," his youngest brother announced, spreading his hands grandly and nearly spilling his coffee again.

Ames was sorely regretting ever confiding in him. "Nobody invited you, brat."

"Not true." Flint carefully set down his mug. "I distinctly

recall you saying you're on your way to the Peppermint Palace this morning to serve as Laura's pickup rider."

"Yes. Alone." It was all Ames could do not to curl his lip in disgust every time he heard the overly Christmassy sounding name of the restaurant spoken out loud. *Only in Pinetop.* Nearly every avenue in town was decorated to a postcard worthy level. The shop owners kept their holiday lights up year round, and so did a good number of the residents. Their constant display of Christmas spirit bordered on ridiculous.

Flint squared his shoulders. "If you can name a single rodeo we've ridden in that's employed less than two pickup riders, then I'll stand down. Otherwise, I'm coming with."

Ames glared at him, starting to feel boxed in. "Are you really that bored?" The last thing he needed was for his youngest brother to tag along, clowning around and creating scenes like he was so fond of doing. Fading into the background was a foreign concept to an attention hog like him.

Flint's expression grew obstinate. "If what you say is true about her being *the one*, it's my future sister-in-law I'll be helping out this morning. Like it or not, I've got some skin in this game."

Ames stood and scraped back his stool. "So help me, Flint, if you do anything more at the restaurant than slurp down that cup of coffee you insist I owe you—"

Flint's loud whoop of elation silenced the rest of Ames' warning. Fortunately, he had the sense to leave his mug on the bar before commencing an obnoxious victory jig around the kitchen.

Ames shook his head at him. "Are you going to at least comb out your bed head?"

"Yup." Flint reached up with both hands to run his fingers through the longish blond waves. If anything, he made it worse. He continued his jig across the living room to the front door, where he stepped into the boots he'd kicked off there last night.

Moving to the sofa, he retrieved his Stetson and spun back toward his brother in a courtly bow. "Do I pass inspection?"

Ames followed him, still shaking his head. "Whoever ends up with you is gonna have her work cut out for her."

"Probably. And I've already got the lucky woman picked out." Grinning from ear to ear, Flint started to button his shirt.

I seriously doubt that. His youngest brother reveled way too much in all the attention of the rodeo groupies. Ames had yet to see him go on more than two or three dates with the same woman. He had an awful lot of growing up still to do.

"You missed a button." He reached over to flick the button in question, letting his arm continue swinging upward toward Flint's nose.

Flint neatly dodged the intended nose flick while fixing the button he'd previously missed. Then he stuffed the front flaps of his shirt tails loosely into his jeans. "I'm ready to two-step, darling." He wagged his eyebrows suggestively at Ames' sock feet.

Out of sheer habit, Ames mechanically slung a leg toward the door but encountered nothing but air. He scowled at the empty spot by the door where his boots normally rested. "What did you do with my boots?" *So help me!* Living with Flint could be such a pain in the rear sometimes, and Ames already had more than enough aches and pains radiating from his shoulder blades to his backside — thanks to his skid down the icy porch steps next door.

"They're in the mud room." Flint's voice was deceptively polite and helpful.

"Why?" They were two single guys batching it alone. It

wasn't as if anyone cared how many boots they left by the front door.

"So I could get a head start to the truck in case you tried to stop me from riding shotgun." Flint whipped his jacket from the hall tree and took off at a jog down the stairs leading to their lower-level garage. He banged the door shut behind him. Loudly.

Silently begging the Lord for patience, Ames stomped to the mudroom around the corner to retrieve his boots. It doubled as a laundry room. A washer and dryer rested inside a storage alcove on one side, and a bench with locker room hooks mounted over it filled the space on the other side.

Flint had literally tossed Ames' boots inside the room, probably without even looking. One was perched haphazardly on the edge of the washer. The other boot was lying on its side in the doorway.

Ames was in no mood for conversation by the time he made his way to the truck he'd been sharing with Flint during their stint in Pinetop. If his youngest brother valued his life, he'd pipe down during the short drive to the restaurant.

To his surprise, the garage door was already rolled open, and not one but two brothers awaited him inside the truck. It was a restored, black and silver classic Chevy. One long leather seat filled the cab. There was no console divider.

Ames yanked open the door to the driver's side. "What in the world?" Their oldest brother, Nash, was lounged in the middle of the seat with his bionic arm hiked up on the back of the seat behind Flint. It was downright miraculous how well he'd adjusted to his new life as an amputee.

Flint pushed his Stetson back to fix Ames with an innocent look. "All pickup riders are present and accounted for, sir." He punctuated the claim with a sharp military salute. "We're doing this Carson brothers' style."

Ames glanced at his watch, irritated to see that it was

already quarter 'til eight. There was no time left to argue the matter. He climbed behind the wheel, slammed the door shut, and started the motor.

"Cranky," Flint hissed in a stage voice.

Nash gave him a warning look. "So, uh...Noelle gave me permission to tell you two something and only you two."

Ames's insides tightened with apprehension as he backed from the garage and rolled down the driveway. "Is she okay?"

His oldest brother's expression softened. "She's pregnant."

"Whoa!" Ames feathered the truck brakes for a moment before jamming down on them at the base of the driveway. "Congratulations!" He leaned over to deliver a hug, bumping Stetsons in the process and knocking them askew.

"Thanks!" Nash straightened his hat just in time for Flint to slap his arms around him in an explosive bear hug. This time, Nash's Stetson went flying to his knees.

"I'm gonna be an uncle!" Flint's delighted crow filled the cab.

"You're not the only one." Ames felt a grin pull at his mouth. It was impossible to remain in a grumpy mood in the face of such incredible news.

A little over a year ago, Nash had lost his right arm about an inch above the elbow in a highway accident that had nearly claimed his life. It had been touch and go for a few hours. The following days, weeks, and months had been full of even more challenges for the young bronc champion turned amputee. He'd assumed his rodeo career was over, but that was before the offer to come perform at Castellano's indoor rodeo had arrived in the mail.

Fourteen months later, Nash was straddling two home addresses between Dallas and Pinetop, Arizona — serving as a rodeo rider, ranch manager, brother, husband, and now a father-to-be. He was a living, breathing miracle in cowboy boots. Someone Ames looked up to more than anyone else in the world. After losing their parents in their teens, Nash had also been serving as something of a father figure to Ames and Flint.

Ames continued to steal glances at his oldest brother as he drove them to Pinetop's busiest downtown area. While Flint cracked a steady stream of new uncle jokes, Nash sat there looking genuinely happy. It was nothing less than he and Noelle deserved. The two of them had started off as friends, really good ones, before falling in love. As far as Ames was concerned, they'd set the gold standard for relationships. He could only hope and pray that he and Laura would be able to build something similar on their own incredible friendship.

He was so immersed in his thoughts that he almost missed the turn into the parking lot of the Peppermint Palace. He had to stop the truck and back up a few feet to avoid hitting the curb.

Flint indulged them with the sound of whooshing air brakes, following by the mechanical beeps of a work truck backing up in a construction zone.

"Do you mind?" Ames sent him a dark look.

Flint immediately launched into the sound of police sirens. He made it sound so real that Ames actually ducked a quick glance into his rearview mirror.

"Gotcha, sucker!" Flint pointed at him and burst out laughing.

Ames shook his head at Nash. "You do realize he's gonna be the uncle who buys drum sets, corn poppers, and all the other most annoying toys ever invented?"

Nash chuckled. "Guess it's a good thing we're friends with a family of heirloom toy makers." He elbowed Ames knowingly as he drove across the nearly empty parking lot to claim one of the front row spots. "Maybe you can put a bug in their ears to steer a certain young uncle accordingly?"

"Sure thing on the bug." Ames rolled his eyes. "No promises on the steering. It's Flint we're talking about."

"I'm right here, bros," the brother in question reminded cheerfully.

"Only because you invited yourself," Ames shot back.

"Technically, I invited Nash," Flint corrected with a smirk. "I'm the stowaway you don't think you need, but I'm about to prove you wrong."

"Or," Ames countered testily as he pushed open his door, "you can play the part of a silent observer before I do you bodily harm."

"Eh, what's the fun in that?" Looking unphased by the threat, Flint opened his door and hopped down to the pavement with a jackrabbit sized bounce. "Oh, wait! I know the answer to that question. Without me, you'd have no idea that ex-Romeo is gonna be running a good ten minutes late to the par-tay." He drew out the word playfully. "That's because someone gave him the wrong directions. Oh, and Lucy dropped Laura off right before we pulled up, so she's already waiting inside the building all by her lonesome."

Though Ames didn't know how his youngest brother had scraped up the information about Brex Morrison's arrival time, it didn't take a genius to figure out he'd been talking to Lucy about the last item. With a growl of irritation, he tossed his truck keys to Nash and took off jogging, clearing the peppermint drawbridge in front of the silly looking restaurant well ahead of his brothers. He gritted his teeth as he entered the cylindrical building that had been painted to resemble a gigantic stack of pancakes. It felt like stepping onto the set of a cartoon television show.

Just as Flint had promised, Laura was standing alone in the wide front waiting area. Though cushioned benches lined the walls on three sides of it, she was standing a few feet away from the hostess booth, nervously twisting the corner of her thick cardigan sweater.

When the front door jingled to announce Ames' entrance, she whirled in his direction. "Oh! Hi, Ames!" If anyone had been watching the way her tired expression lit up, they'd have assumed she'd been waiting for him instead of someone else.

He strode her way, ignoring the fact that he was supposed to be remaining in the background. "Hey, you!" He wrapped his arms around her and lifted her to spin her in a full circle. "Fancy running into you here," he teased as he set her down. The shadows beneath her eyes tugged at his heartstrings. It didn't look like she'd gotten any more sleep than he had.

She still looked amazing, though. Forcing his arms back to his sides, he drank her in like a man dying of thirst. Her dark hair was pulled back in a sassy ponytail that made his fingers itch to give it a yank. There was no stopping the low whistle of admiration that escaped him. She looked that good in jeans and boots, something he rarely got to see her in. Most of the time, she was wearing an elf costume, the standard uniform at Santa's Toy Factory where she worked. And unlike last night, her jeans weren't sporting a coffee stain the size of Utah.

She stepped closer to hiss, "Did you just wolf whistle at me, Ames Carson?"

"What if I did?" He gazed down at her for an unguarded moment, allowing her to read everything he was thinking and feeling.

"You look ready to steal that kiss you keep talking about." She gave a breathy giggle and took a step back.

"Darling, I was born ready for that." He winked at her.

"Probably not a good idea to start your life of crime this morning." She whirled to face the front door as it jingled again, instinctively backing up a step in his direction.

He doubted she'd even realized what she'd done. It made

his heart sing to know she felt safe with him. He bent to speak directly in her ear. "Relax. It's just my brothers."

She slumped in relief against him, briefly tipping her head against his chest. He wanted so badly to hold her that it was all he could do to keep his arms at his sides. However, Brex Morrison could walk in at any moment.

As Nash strode closer, she sprang forward to wrap him in a gentle hug. "Congratulations, Nash! I'm so happy for you and Noelle."

Nash gave Ames a wide-eyed look of accusation over her head.

Ames spread his hands, silently protesting his innocence. There was no way he would've spilled a secret like that without his brother's permission, not even to Laura.

She stepped back with an apologetic smile. "I know I'm probably not supposed to know, but it's a small town, and..." She gave a helpless shrug. "One person saw Noelle leaving the doctor's office yesterday. Someone else caught her browsing through baby clothes at one of the boutiques, and yet another person claims she was looking pale around the gills over her salmon salad at the Gingerbread House. With that many nosy locals, it was impossible not to connect the dots."

Nash snorted out a laugh. "Yeah, that's Pinetop for you." He didn't look too bothered by it. The place was clearly growing on him. It was growing on all of them. "To keep me out of trouble with my wife, I won't pass on your congratulations. Instead, I'll let you deliver them yourself the next time you see her."

"I can't wait! This is so exciting!" Laura clasped her gloved hands together, dancing her gaze over the three of them. "So, what are the odds of running into all three of you here this morning?" To her credit, she sounded really happy about it.

When none of them leaped forward with an answer, she nodded in understanding. "I'm getting the whole pickup riding team, aren't I?" The look she sent over her shoulder at Ames was brimming with gratitude.

"We've got your back, just like I promised." He winked at her.

A tinge of pink blossomed across her high cheekbones. "I really owe you for this."

"Yeah, you do," he teased, "and I intend to collect." It would be the perfect time for her to pay up with that kiss they continued to joke about privately.

The color in her face deepened.

Flint cleared his throat and muttered, "Go time." As smooth as if he'd rehearsed the maneuver, he two-stepped around Laura, cutting ahead of her in line at the hostess station. "Reservation for Flint, party of three," he intoned in a low voice.

"You little punk," Ames growled, half swinging in his direction. However, he was careful to keep the front entrance door in his peripheral vision until it opened.

The infamous Gypsy Boy, who'd so callously broken Laura's heart, strutted in like a rooster ready to crow at the crack of dawn. His homespun appearance was the antithesis of the bounce in his step. His double-breasted wool jacket was clearly one he'd purchased second-hand, probably from some military clothing outlet. It was unbuttoned, revealing a neck scarf, a denim shirt with the collar casually pushed up, and yet another scarf on top of that. It was secured by a square antique pin. His hands were bare, revealing a trail of floral and bird tattoos. He was really playing up the gypsy look.

Though his dark hair was windblown, it had recently been cut, possibly by hand since it looked a little uneven over his right ear. Either that, or he'd carelessly shoved it back before entering the restaurant. He was sporting an evening shadow that was quickly working its way into a beard. His entire appearance felt deliberate. Staged. Something that belonged on the cover of a movie magazine.

Ames reckoned he should've expected no less from a man with an agenda, one that clearly involved the woman whose life he was attempting to slither back into.

"Laura." Brex Morrison's voice held a curious mix of raspy emotion and regret, probably something he'd practiced. "It's so good to see you again."

Her expression tightened. Whatever he'd hoped to accomplish with his dramatic entrance into the restaurant had failed to hit its mark. "We need to talk." She made no move to shake the hand he was holding out to her.

He lowered it with a wistful sigh. "That's why I'm here."

"If you'll follow me, sir." The hostess lightly touched Ames' shoulder to get his attention. "Your table is ready."

Right. He mechanically followed her from the waiting area, keeping his head averted so he could continue discreetly observing Laura and her breakfast companion. The hostess led him and his brothers to a table against the east side of the room. A padded bench was built into the wall on one side of the table, and two chairs were pushed up to the other side of it.

Flint angled his head at the bench. "You get first dibs on the wall, bro."

"Thanks." Ames took a seat, liking the central location of their table. It gave him a full view of the rest of the room.

"I specifically requested this table." Flint slid in beside him. "So I hope that's your way of saying you owe me more than a coffee, especially since I left my wallet at home."

"Of course you did." Ames' gaze never left the entrance of the dining room, which the hostess soon led Laura and Brex through. To his surprise, she seated them at the table right across from him and his brothers.

Laura's startled gaze briefly fluttered to him.

He gave her what he hoped she would interpret as an encouraging nod.

She either didn't notice or purposely ignored the chair her ex-fiancé held for her. Instead, she pulled out her own chair, the one facing Ames.

That's right, darling. You need anything, and I'll be right here.

Flint opened his menu and spoke in a low voice from behind it. "You're mighty welcome for the view, bro. If they served steak for breakfast, this meal would be costing you a lot more."

Their waitress arrived with complimentary glasses of water. Handing out straws, she lifted her pen over her pad to take their orders. "What'll it be for you guys this morning?"

Nash ripped the paper off one end of his straw and sent the other end zinging over the top of Flint's menu.

Flint raised a single eyebrow at Ames. "I might've failed to brief him on the all work and no play part of this gig."

CHAPTER 4: TOO LITTLE, TOO LATE

Brex's dark gaze surveyed Laura warily as he claimed the seat beside her, the one he'd originally pulled out for her. She would've preferred it if he'd sat across from her. It felt harder to breathe having him this close.

"I'm sorry." He shook his head at her in a sad puppy kind of way. "I'm going to keep apologizing until you forgive me."

"I forgave you a long time ago." She hated the tremor in her voice and hoped he didn't notice it. Now wasn't the time to dissolve into hysterics. She needed answers.

"Thank you. It's more than I deserve." Reaching into one of his large coat pockets, he withdrew a delicate wooden flower and laid it on the table between them. Though it looked handcrafted, she doubted it was his work. He'd never commanded that kind of finesse with a set of carving tools.

Back when they were dating, a gift like that would've melted her heart into a puddle of liquid on the floor. At the moment, she found herself simply wondering why he'd bothered.

She raised her gaze to him without acknowledging his gift. "Why did you ask to see me?"

"Are you kidding?" His eyes widened in a brand of surprise that looked real. "Seeing you is all I've been able to think about since the moment you...since we..." He fell silent, looking uncomfortable.

"You're the one who broke our engagement," she reminded stiffly. *Don't you dare try to rewrite the past on that one, mister!*

"I did, and it's something I will always regret." He dragged in a heavy breath. "And if you hadn't left the circuit shortly afterward, I would've already done a better job of making my regret known to you."

She nodded instead of answering, not sure if he'd intended to make it sound like she owed him an apology for that. Her entire family had moved. It was a business decision that had nothing whatsoever to do with their failed engagement. The fact that he hadn't tried to stop her from moving to Pinetop had been her first clue that he was getting cold feet about their forthcoming marriage. The fact that it had taken more than a year for him to chase after her to attempt a reconciliation was equally concerning.

A waitress approached their table. She set a pair of water glasses on their table with a flourish. "Would you like coffee to go with that? Or tea? Or juice?"

"Coffee, please," Laura murmured. "With cream."

"Make that two coffees," Brex chimed in. "Extra cream for hers."

"You betcha! I'll be right back with them."

A wave of sadness washed over Laura as she watched the waitress sail away to fill their orders. It would've been easier to remain angry with Brex if he'd come back into her life without an apology. Instead, he was making every effort to come across as the same super sweet and sensitive guy she'd first fallen for. It made her wonder all over again where they'd gone wrong in their relationship. What was it about their engagement that had given him cold feet? Why had he ended it so abruptly? And why was he so interested in rekindling it? Why now? What had changed? The more she thought about it, the less sense his sudden reappearance in her life was making.

His mention of her exit from the traveling vendor circuit felt significant. Did he really see that as the reason their relationship had failed? He was referring, of course, to their nomadic existence on the road. For years, her family had fallen into the pattern of traveling the same path and schedule as several other craftsmen and their families. They'd driven from town to town in a caravan of trucks, vans, and RVs. Like their own little tribe. Or band of gypsies, as a few of them preferred to call themselves.

Brex Morrison was one of those people. He'd taken it a step further, more specifically referring to himself as the *Last of the Gypsies*. Not only was it his choice of lifestyle, it was the brand name he'd given the line of merchandise he made and sold. In the end, perhaps it was his gypsy heart that had spelled doom for their almost marriage.

He was a rolling stone with an adventurous soul. He'd continued to wander from town to town and state to state after he'd broken their engagement. Maybe wandering was in his blood. She and her family, on the other hand, were finished with that life. They were very much enjoying having a hometown and a street address. They also greatly appreciated the steady income that came along with it. She had zero interest in returning to Brex Morrison's gypsy existence.

Drawing a bracing breath, she tossed out her next question. "What do you hope to accomplish during your visit to Pinetop?"

"Other than running my booth at the Sweetheart Spectacular?" His dark eyebrows rose. "I'm going to do everything I can to win you back, Laura." He'd started talking almost before she'd finished asking her question. Was it her imagination, or did his answer sound rehearsed?

He hitched his chair closer to hers. "I screwed up, Laura. Letting you go was the worst decision I've ever made. If you can find it in your heart to give me another chance, I want to show you that I've changed. That I'm capable of continuing to change for you." He pressed both hands dramatically to his heart. "For us."

Us? She stared aghast at him. *There's no us any longer.* Despite how prettily he was begging, there was no answering spark inside of her. She was, however, suddenly and acutely more aware of Ames Carson's presence at the table across from theirs. She could feel his gaze on her and sense his support. She clung to the feeling like it was a lifeline.

"Say something, Laura." Brex ducked his head, attempting to bring them eye to eye.

However, she leaned away from him, repulsed by the thought of sharing that kind of intimacy with him again. The realization slammed into her that it was over between them. Truly over.

The waitress returned with their coffees, breaking the awkward silence that had followed his impassioned plea. "What else can I bring you two sweeties?"

Sweeties? Ugh! Laura shook her head. "Coffee is more than enough. Thank you. I'm not hungry."

A wrinkle formed in the middle of Brex's forehead. It was the first sign of irritation he'd shown since walking into the restaurant. "Of course, we're eating! That's the whole reason we agreed to a breakfast date." He rattled off a request for a double order of biscuits with sausage gravy. "And a side of fresh fruit," he finished with a sly wink at Laura. "Her favorite."

Her eyes widened in dismay at him. Did he honestly consider this to be a date? That he could simply march back into her life after being gone for over a year and simply pick up where they'd left off?

Brex waited until the waitress walked away before grumbling, "Quit looking at me like that. You know how much I've always hated making scenes in public." He glanced furtively around them at the quickly filling dining room. The Peppermint Palace was a popular breakfast venue in Pinetop. The locals and tourists alike were avid patrons of their art-like culinary creations, as well as the handful of peppermints they piled on every ticket at the end.

Her anger sparked at his tone. He was acting like she was a small child in need of a reprimand. She'd all but forgotten about this side of him — his condescending streak that coiled like a cobra in the shadows and struck without warning. No, he hadn't changed. Growing a short beard and tossing a few carefully rehearsed apologies into her lap didn't qualify as meaningful change.

"What I think," she said slowly, fighting to keep her temper under control, "is that you and I came into this *meeting* with very different goals in mind." She reached for the wristlet lying on the table beside her. Unzipping the pocket where she kept her cash, she withdrew a few dollar bills and laid them on the table. It was more than enough to cover her cup of coffee. "I was looking for closure about a marriage that almost happened, but didn't. Not..." She waved a hand vaguely in his direction, "whatever you seem to think this is."

"Reconciliation," he supplied in a mildly sarcastic voice. His veneer of humble remorse was quickly slipping. "Couples do it all the time. They work out their differences and come out stronger on the other side."

She shot to her feet so quickly that she nearly knocked over her chair. It scooted back with a noisy scraping sound. "Number one, we are not a couple. Number two, this is not a breakfast date." Her voice crescendoed as she met Ames' bemused gaze, well aware that the rising volume of her voice was making heads turn in their direction. "Number three, I'm walking out of here before you get schooled on what an actual scene looks like."

He shook his head in disappointment at her. "I still enjoyed seeing you again, Laura. Maybe we can visit again before I leave town?" He glanced around them again, his mouth twisting in distaste at the growing crowd. "Maybe somewhere a little more private?" His condescending tone was back.

A huff of disbelief escaped her. "I don't see the point since I have nothing more to say to you. This was a mistake. Goodbye, Brex." She yanked her jacket off the back of her chair and spun blindly away from him.

And nearly smacked into Ames.

"Whoa there!" He gently caught her elbows. "Oh, hey, Laura!" He pretended like he was just then recognizing her. "What's going on? Are you alright?" The look he gave Brex was drenched in frost.

"Yes. I, er…" she slid from his grasp and stumbled past him, "just remembered I need to take care of something important at work."

He stalked after her. "You need a ride?"

She didn't answer until they were standing outside the restaurant. She fumbled with her jacket, shivering uncontrollably. "Th-that was a very bad idea!" She scowled back at the restaurant.

Ames quickly moved behind her to hold up her jacket so she could slide her arms into it. "Come on." While she zipped up her jacket, he slung an arm around her shoulders. "You're freezing. Let's get you out of here."

She twisted her head around, trying to see if his brothers were following them. "What about Nash and Flint?"

"Don't worry about them." He tugged her tighter against

his side. "Flint will be more than happy to eat the pancakes I ordered. I'll text him and Nash to let them know I'll come back for them in a bit." He led her to his gorgeous old Chevy, unlocked the driver's door, and gave her a boost into his seat.

"Aren't you hungry?" She had to grit her teeth to stop them from chattering as she shimmied over to make room for him.

"Yep, but I can eat later. Right now, I'm more interested in getting you out of here." He leaped into the seat beside her, scowling in concern down at her. "Because that's what pickup riders are for."

His raw sincerity was so refreshing that she burst into tears. Until this very moment, it hadn't dawned on her that everything he'd ever said to her could be taken at face value. With him, there was no guessing. Nothing but pure, unadulterated honesty and kindness.

"Hey, that wasn't supposed to make you cry!" He sounded agonized as he slammed his door shut and started the motor. Reaching toward the dashboard, he turned on the heater and aimed the central vent at her.

"I know." She fumbled with her seatbelt and was relieved when he took over and snapped it into place. "Sorry. I'm just...overwhelmed right now."

"That's understandable." He tightened the strap a little to make it more secure. "Listen, if you want to talk about what happened back there, I'm a good listener. If you don't wanna talk, I'm also good at cranky silence. Just ask Flint." He glanced over his shoulder before pulling out of his parking spot. He paused at the parking lot exit, popping on his right blinker.

Too many emotions to name bubbled inside her. "I should've n-never suggested meeting for b-breakfast," she confessed through chattering teeth. "From the m-moment we sat down, he acted like it was a d-date."

With a grunt that she couldn't quite interpret, Ames slung an arm across the seat behind her. "Yeah, that's a little strange, considering how long it's been since you last saw each other."

She tipped her head against his well-corded arm. "I still don't understand why he bothered coming into town. I may never understand it."

"Did you ask him?" Ames sounded puzzled as he turned onto Main Street and cruised slowly toward Santa's Toy Factory.

"I did." She frowned at his strong jawline. "He gave me some cock and bull story about wanting to get back together."

"Not surprised about that." Ames' voice was dry.

"Well, I am," she exploded. "He dodged the question both times I tried to drill down into why he broke up with me in the first place. If he's not willing to even discuss where we went wrong, I don't see any path forward for us." Quite frankly, she'd lost interest in even hunting for a path forward.

"Breaking my heart." Ames gave her a squeeze hug.

"No, it's not." She burrowed closer to him, finally starting to warm up. "And it's one of the things I appreciate the most about you."

"Oh, really?" He sounded fascinated.

"You're so stinking honest. I don't have to second-guess every word that comes out of your mouth to try to figure out what you really mean."

"Yep, I'm a what you see is what you get kinda guy, right down to the endless quantities of spilled coffee." He turned into the parking lot of the toy store.

She squirmed on the seat cushion, realizing he didn't get that she'd made up her excuse about needing to get back to work. She only worked every other Saturday. "So, um, today is actually my day off," she confessed as he pulled around back and brought his truck to a halt in front of the rear exit.

"I am aware." He set the emergency brake and swiveled her way without killing the motor.

"Then why did you bring me here?" She raised her head to take in their surroundings and discovered that the sporty white Jeep she shared with her sister was the only other vehicle parked back there. She and Ames were otherwise alone, sandwiched between the three-story toy store and the mountain behind them.

"To regroup." He cocked his head at her. "Sometimes you need a moment to just breathe after a big performance in the ring."

"Thank you for understanding." She smiled shyly at him.

He responded with a lazy grin that made her heartbeat pick up the pace a little. "You feeling any better?"

"A little." Her smile slipped as she replayed the events from the past half hour or so inside her head. "Brex's sudden appearance in town is nagging at me. Something feels off about it." Several somethings, actually. If he was truly interested in reconciliation, it had taken him an awfully long time to come to that decision. And why show up without giving her advance notice? Signing up for the Sweetheart Spectacular felt off, too. In the past, he and his gypsy craftsmen friends hadn't given small towns like this a second glance, preferring to spend their time and resources on bigger cities that drew much larger crowds.

Ames drummed his fingers against her shoulder. "You care to elaborate on that?"

"I'll try." She scrambled to put her worries and fears into words. "If Brex Morrison's goal really is to win me back, he did too little too late."

Ames' expression lit. "I can certainly get on board with that statement."

"And I really don't get why he bothered signing up for the Sweetheart Spectacular. In the past, he avoided small towns like the plague."

"You're here," Ames pointed out mildly.

"I've been here for over a year," she reminded.

"There's that." His hand tightened around her shoulder.

"What if he had another reason for coming to town?" she mused. He'd always been a bit on the mysterious side, sometimes conversing like old friends with men and women she'd never laid eyes on before. She'd always credited it to his ability to make friends quickly, but what if there was more to the seedy company he sometimes kept?

"I don't know." Ames shook his head. "Want me to ask around to see if anyone else can help shed light on that?"

"If it's not too much trouble. I'll do the same." She bit down on her lower lip. "All we really know, at this point, is that he has a booth reserved at the Valentine craft fair. I'm not even sure what he's peddling these days." Her thoughts returned to the delicate wooden flower he'd laid on the table at the Peppermint Palace.

"Toys," Ames supplied.

She eyed him curiously. "How do you know that?"

"Because I have a very nosy younger brother." He gave her a wry look. "Between last night and this morning, he took it upon himself to play Sherlock and do some digging around. So did Flash Billings." At her puzzled expression, he explained, "The guy who gives all the sleigh rides around town."

"Oh, he was a sweetheart!" She was really looking forward to taking him up on his offer to reschedule their sleigh ride.

"You might've seen him at the post office, too, where he proudly serves as postmaster." His lips quirked. "Often in holiday attire."

"Now that you mention it..." Laura's mother usually made

the daily post office run for the Merry Woodmakers, but Laura had gone in her place a few times.

A contemplative silence settled between them. It didn't take long, though, for more questions to start burning inside her.

"Do you know what kind of toys Brex brought with him to sell?" She was dying to know if he was working solo these days, or if he intended to display a conglomeration of products from other crafters. He'd often done so in the past, usually for the seedy new friends he'd made in nearly every town they'd visited.

"On his application for a booth, he stated that he sells children's toys. Wooden ones. Sounded a lot like what you and your family make."

"Not even close!" She shook her head vehemently. "He makes quirky stuff, like slingshots and rubber band guns. He gets a lot of complaints from parents over safety issues." Brex generally brushed off their concerns, calling them helicopter parents who were afraid of letting their kids have a little fun. He liked to brag that slingshots and guns were some of the most beloved toys of all time. Once, he'd even drawn a Biblical reference to the story of David killing Goliath with a slingshot.

Ames grunted. "There was no mention of that in the description he gave for his products. I think the exact word he used on his application was heirloom. Yeah, that's it. He said he makes heirloom toys."

Laura's lips parted in shock. "That's how my family has always described our toys. In the past, he focused on the gypsy theme of his products when filling out applications."

"Guess he's switched up his game." Ames didn't sound any more thrilled about it than she was.

"It's a complete knock-off of our branding, if you ask me," she spluttered. Her parents were going to be sad and disappointed all over again about her ex. Lucy might take it a step further, hunt him down, and try to wring his neck.

"It'll be interesting to see what shakes out when I ask around town about this chucklehead." Ames reluctantly straightened, pulling his arm off the seat behind her and reaching for the steering wheel. "In the meantime, let me know where you want me to drop you off. My brothers are probably finished eating by now and wondering when I'm going to show back up."

She drew a deep breath and let it out. "I should probably stay here and go check on my sister."

He raised his eyebrows at her. "I thought you said—"

"I know." She made a face at him. "Now that I've thawed out, I've changed my mind. Work is exactly what I need to throw myself into after what just happened. Plus, Lucy is probably dying to hear all about it while it's hot off the grill. Paying her a visit will save my texting fingers." She wiggled them in the air at him. "I'll catch a ride home with her."

His gaze lingered on her face for a moment. "If you're sure you're sure."

"I'm sure." She impulsively touched his arm. "Thanks for everything. Tell your brothers I said thanks to them, too. You guys are the best pickup riders!"

"Our pleasure, ma'am." Ames punctuated his words with a devilish wink. Then he opened his door and leaped to the ground. Turning around, he held out his arms for her.

She unclasped her seatbelt and scooted closer. Then she slowly leaned into his arms.

As he lowered her to the ground, their gazes clashed and held.

"Ames." His name tore out of her. "I..." As if drawn by a magnet, her gaze shifted to his hard mouth. It was the first time she'd allowed her mind to go there, to think about kissing her best friend.

His eyelids grew heavier. "You want to know what it's like, too, don't you?"

She caught her lower lip between her teeth with a bleat of distress, yanking her gaze back up to his. *What am I doing?*

His blue eyes burned knowingly into hers. "It's okay to admit you want to kiss me, Laura. Your secrets are safe with me. All of them."

"I don't know what to say," she whispered. Yes, she wanted to kiss him. No, she wasn't ready for things to change between them like that. What if it didn't work? What if it destroyed their beautiful friendship? She wasn't sure her heart could handle being shattered a second time.

He rubbed his hands up and down her arms. "You don't have to say anything yet. Just keep thinking about it." He drew her closer, dipping his head over hers to bring their mouths nearer. "About us. About what it's gonna feel like when we finally take that leap." He reached up to brush his thumb across her cheek. "Together."

She finally found the strength to move again. "Okay, Ames." She reluctantly slid from his grasp. "I'll think about it, okay?"

"So will I." He tipped his hat at her.

She could feel his gaze on her while she moved toward the rear entrance to Santa's Toy Factory. And while she fumbled with her key in the lock. Unable to resist, she glanced back at him before pushing the door open and letting herself inside.

He was lounged against his truck, arms folded, eyes glinting possessively at her.

Catching her breath, she hurried inside and shut the door. Leaning back against it, she closed her eyes. "Oh, my goodness! That just happened," she whispered into the empty hallway.

"What just happened?" Her younger sister's voice jolted

her from the delicious haze her thoughts had become tangled in.

Laura jolted in surprise, eyelids flying upward. "I thought I was alone."

"Clearly." Lucy's dark eyes sparkled with mischief. She tossed a handful of her long, ice-white hair over her shoulder. For the past couple of years, she'd been dyeing her hair blonde. Though she refused to admit it, Laura was convinced it was because she was tired of them being confused as twins. They still looked a lot alike, even with Lucy's drastically different hair color.

Her younger sister danced closer. Since she was on the clock, she was in her elf costume. "Did you finally kiss him?" Her felt hat and striped stockings enhanced the wickedness painted across her expression.

Laura gasped. Were her thoughts really that transparent? "Wh-what are you talking about?"

"Ames Carson. Who else?"

Laura swallowed hard. "You do realize I went to breakfast with Brex Morrison?"

"According to the security camera in the back parking lot, you came back with Ames."

"Oh, now you're spying on me?" Laura couldn't believe what she was hearing.

"If I was, I wouldn't have to ask if you finally put the guy out of his misery and puckered up for him."

"Not even!" She squared her shoulders, pretending indignance. "We're only friends."

Lucy rolled her eyes. "The lies we tell ourselves," she sighed.

"I don't ever want to lose his friendship," Laura said quickly. "Or him."

Lucy's wicked look vanished. "He's pretty special, isn't he?"

Laura nodded, eyes misting. "I don't know what I would've done without him this morning." She didn't want to even think about it. "He's always been there for me, Luce. He's always had my back. I...I trust him." She drew a breath and let it out. "Completely."

Lucy's smile grew poignant. "In case I haven't made myself clear, I really, really, really like the way he treats my sister. You deserve to have a guy in your life who puts you first." Her expression darkened. "Unlike your arrogant, vainglorious, narcissistic toad of an ex!"

"Lucy!" Laura stepped away from the door, wide-eyed. "I had no idea you despised him so much."

"Oh, I was never all that impressed with him." Lucy's mouth twisted in distaste. "But after what he did to you, my opinion of him went downhill like an avalanche." She balled a hand into a fist and socked it into her other hand. "Dare I ask how your breakfast with him went?" She took a few steps backward and waved Laura into the nearest office. It was the one they shared.

Toy designs and patterns were scattered across both chrome desks. Organization had never been their strong point. Creativity was.

Laura spread her hands. "He claims he wants me back." Saying it out loud didn't make it sound any more convincing. She was harboring some serious doubts about his true agenda.

"And?" Lucy waved impatiently for her to continue. Sweeping a stack of papers off her desk onto the floor, she hopped up on it and patted the spot beside her.

Laura joined her, swinging her legs a little to stretch them. "I felt nothing."

"That's a good thing!" Lucy clapped her hands excitedly. Then she cocked her head at Laura. "Right?"

Laura wasn't sure how to put what she was feeling into words. "I went into it looking for closure about where we went wrong as a couple, but he refused to give me a straight answer about anything. About why he broke up. About whether he was ever going to be ready to leave the circuit. And then..." She glanced away. "It hit me that it no longer mattered, because he no longer matters. Not to me."

"Oh, honey!" Lucy impulsively threw an arm around her, leaning closer to tip their heads together. "I'm sorry you had to deal with all that this morning, but I'm not too terribly torn up about how it ended."

"Me, either," Laura assured. "Really." It was a relief to admit it out loud. "I think this means I'm finally over him." It had been a long, rocky path full of tears and heartache to reach this point.

"I'm glad." Lucy hugged her tighter. "Now if we could circle back to the other topic." Her smile flashed to its high-beam setting. "Are you ever going to get around to kissing Ames Carson?"

CHAPTER 5: WHAT COULD'VE BEEN

Five days later

The citizens of Pinetop were experts at hosting and welcoming people from all over the globe to their holiday craft fairs. The Sweetheart Spectacular was no exception. The decorating committee had gone all out on the Valentine-themed exhibits inside the largest, multi-purpose room at the Pinetop Civic Center.

There was a Queen of Hearts selfie station, inspired by the Alice in Wonderland movie. There was also a Cinderella carriage with real horses, a uniformed driver, and liveried footmen to pose beside. Everywhere Ames looked there were hearts, roses, balloons, and red. Lots and lots of red.

He strolled between the rows of craft booths, enjoying the sights and sounds more than he'd expected. He found himself grinning at a collection of life-sized cardboard cutouts of various celebrity couples. Where their faces had been were empty holes for people to pose behind — everyone from beloved sports champions to royalty.

Though he was still getting used to the constant holiday

celebrations that Pinetop was so famous for, he could easily picture Laura in a setting like this. She'd be in her element behind a craft booth. She and her family adored the holidays.

He tried not to make eye contact with the vendors. Each time he did by accident, he was offered a sample of fudge, jellies, chip dips, soups, and beverages. A trio of clowns mingled with the crowd, offering to blow up long, brightly colored balloons that they twisted into various creatures — dogs, monkeys, butterflies, snails, snakes, and even a frog.

Keeping his head down, Ames reached the end of the second row of booths and rounded the corner to examine what was being sold on the third line. Though he'd passed by a few dozen booths already, he'd yet to reach the one he was looking for.

According to the trifold map of the event he'd been handed at the entrance doors, Brex Morrison's booth should've been in the children's products section at station ninety-six. For this reason, Ames had been browsing his way through the craft fair in reverse order. Station ninety-six, however, was hosting a finger painting station — not Brex's heirloom toys.

He silently counted off the number signs posted in front of each booth. Fifty-six, fifty-five, fifty-four... At station fifty-two, he entered a section displaying handmade toiletries. Candles flickered, and the scent of newly cut bars of soaps and hand lotions filled the air. It was an eclectic mix of smells. Not bad, actually. Still no Brex Morrison, though.

The jewelry booths were next.

Wow! Ames shoved his hands deeper in the pockets of his jeans, stifling a low whistle at the glitter of gems catching the morning sunlight. There were diamonds, rubies, emeralds, and amethysts.

And Brex.

He was manning a booth right in the middle of it all.

Ames slowed his steps to a shuffle, sweeping the contents of Brex's table from beneath the brim of his Stetson. It was odd seeing a toy booth in the middle of a bunch of jewelry booths. Not that there was any law against it.

What he saw on display at Brex's table brought him to a halt. The wooden snowmen nutcrackers scattered across a sheet of white Poly-fil definitely qualified as heirloom toys. Other than the fact that they were snowmen, they were eerily similar to the festive Santas Laura had designed for the Merry Woodmakers' line of nutcrackers.

Ames had stood inside the back of Santa's Toy Factory enough times, watching her parents through the glass as they painstakingly carved, painted, and glued the exquisite creatures together.

Like Laura's festive Santas, Brex's snowmen bore custom hats, gloves, and other accessories. Ames froze at the sight of a tiny rabbit perched on the tree stick arm of one of the snowmen. It looked like an exact replica of one of the miniature rabbits he'd recently witnessed Ayaka Lee gluing onto one of their festive Santas.

He took a step closer to the table, finally realizing how Brex had managed to get his booth moved to the jewelry section of the craft fair. The squatty lower half of his snowmen nutcrackers held an additional detail. The lowest of their three buttons doubled as a pull-down handle, revealing a hidden compartment. The space could be used to hide valuables — small ones like wedding rings, earrings, brooches, or bracelets. The one on display was open, revealing a diamond ring resting inside it.

"Hey! Didn't I see you at the Peppermint Palace the other day?" Brex Morrison's voice wafted his way, making Ames realize it would be impossible to avoid an encounter. Part of him was glad. He wanted to look the guy in the eye and peel back the layers of what he was up to.

He took his time raising his head, pretending to glance around him in an effort to locate the owner of the voice. Finally swiveling in Brex's direction, he exclaimed, "Oh, hi. Yeah, I remember seeing you there. You're Laura's friend, aren't you?"

Brex's swarthy features were unsmiling. "I was going to ask you the same thing." He stretched out one hand airily. "Friend?" He stretched out the other hand. "Or taxi driver?"

Ames was mildly amused by the toy maker's attempt to get under his skin. However, he'd pumped so much adrenaline from the backs of so many spirited broncos that it was no longer easy to get him riled up. He'd taken falls, hits, and kicks. He'd broken plenty of bones. Learning how to keep a cool head through it all, time after time, was what had allowed him to live to see another day.

"Both, I guess." He boldly held the man's gaze. "I'm whatever Laura needs me to be." He had no problem letting Brex Morrison know he was her biggest ally. If the guy was up to no good, maybe it would give him second thoughts before trying anything stupid.

He was dressed in full gypsy mode again today, with lots of rings, beads, scarves, and layers. At close range, Ames was pretty sure the guy's carefully tousled hair was held in place by hairspray. What a fraud! He could call himself a gypsy all he wanted, but he was a little too GQ perfect about the details to come across as authentic.

The craftsman cocked his head to study Ames slyly. "Don't bother getting your hopes up in her direction, bronc rider. She's not going to leave her family. Not for you, me, or anyone else. So unless you plan on relocating permanently to this remote speck of a town..." He shrugged and dropped his hands.

Apparently, Brex had done his homework. It sounded like he knew what the Carson brothers did for a living. *Interesting.*

It would be even more interesting to find out whether he'd done his homework on them before or after his arrival to Pinetop.

"Haven't decided," Ames drawled. It was the truth. "It all depends on what the Lord has in store for me and my family." He pointed upward. "We lean towards letting Him call the shots." That was the strategy that had gotten them through the loss of their parents, as well as the partial amputation of Nash's right arm. They always discussed things first as a family, prayed for direction, then made their decisions together.

They'd come up with this strategy after hearing a sermon about the fourth chapter of Ecclesiastes.

Two are better than one, because they have a good return for their labor. If either of them falls down, one can help the other up. But pity anyone who falls and has no one to help them up...

Though one may be overpowered, two can defend themselves. A cord of three strands is not quickly broken.

Ames and his brothers had decided years ago that the three of them were stronger together than apart. They'd joined the rodeo circuit together and made a name for themselves as bronc riding champions. After packing away enough winning pots and buckles, they'd subsequently purchased Canyon Creek Ranch together. And after Nash's injury, they'd transferred to Castellano's indoor rodeo together. Being a team worked for them. He didn't see that changing anytime soon.

Brex made a disparaging sound. "Ah. You're one of *those*." His tone indicated that he thought Ames was some crazy religious fanatic, the kind with less than all of his brain cells intact.

Ames regarded him sagely. "Nah, I just like to keep things simple." He moved his hands in imitation of what Brex had done to him earlier. "You know...right or wrong. Honest or dishonest. Faithful or unfaithful." He paused to let that last point sink in.

Brex's face turned a mottled red. "If you know Laura at all, then you're already aware of the fact that she's a complicated woman. Naturally, our relationship is complicated."

Ames didn't see her that way at all. She'd been hurt, and that hurt had made her cautious. It was as simple as that. He didn't see any reason to argue the matter further with her ex-fiancé, though. He'd already made his point. The guy had blown it with Laura. On some level, he had to know that. If he truly intended to talk her into giving him a second chance, he had an uphill battle ahead. A very steep, very rocky one that wasn't likely to lead where he hoped it would.

"Good talk." Ames glanced pointedly down at the snowmen nutcrackers that Laura had so adamantly insisted were knock-offs of her family's products. "I'll be sure to let her know I ran into you. No doubt she'll want to come take a look at your snowmen for old-time's sake."

It was so subtle that Ames almost missed it, but Brex winced a little. "Yeah, that would be great."

He was lying. Ames had been around long enough to know when someone wasn't being straight with him. *And you think I'm the crazy one? I'm not the one lying to myself.* He almost pitied the guy.

Another glance at the knock-off nutcrackers, however, erased that pity. He had no respect whatsoever for thieves. He intended to inform the Lees, then tip off the event organizers. It wasn't going to break his heart one bit if they gave the guy the boot over his dishonesty.

❄

THURSDAYS WERE LAURA'S FAVORITE DAY OF THE WEEK FOR one simple reason. All four of the Lee toy makers were on duty at the same time. That meant her parents were in the glassed-in workshop in the back of the store, making and decorating toys, while Lucy manned the floor to assist customers. That left Laura free to sit at her easel, sketching out new toy designs.

Sometimes customers watched over her shoulders and asked questions, but they mostly left her alone with her flow of creative juices. Mornings were the quietest, allowing her to get the lion's share of her work done. The afternoons were busier, so she often ended up laying down her pencil or charcoal to assist her sister on the showroom floor.

While she sketched this morning, she allowed her mind to wander. Her thoughts inevitably ended up on her evolving relationship with Ames. She was still getting used to the idea of him being more than a friend. They weren't dating yet, but they'd grown a lot closer in recent days.

She blushed at the memory of his confession about wanting to kiss her. He'd always been honest with her. It was one of his most endearing traits. She hoped he never changed.

She also kind of hoped he'd eventually get around to stealing that kiss he'd been teasing her about lately. Just thinking about it made the heat rise to her cheeks. The way he'd stepped closer and lowered his mouth over hers without quite touching her—

"Nice farm animals."

Ames' husky voice shattered her daydream, making her jump. "Oh, my goodness! I didn't hear you walk up," she gasped, nearly dropping the piece of charcoal she was holding. Glancing to her right, she found him staring in fascination at her latest brainstorm, a set of farm toys. It would consist of wooden animals, a barn that could be constructed piece by piece and taken apart again and again, and fence slats that clipped together and could be arranged in any size or shape of pasture a child wanted. It all depended on how many spare parts their parents would be willing to purchase. The set could be added to throughout the year with holiday themed pieces — bunnies and chickens for Easter, angels and lambs for Christmas, and so on.

"Yeah, you seemed to be in the zone. Sorry to interrupt." He rocked back on the heels of his cowboy boots, giving her an indulgent once-over.

She was immediately ensnared by the warmth and adoration in his eyes. "It's alright. It's always nice to see you."

"Nice?" His eyebrows shot upward. Stepping closer to her, he muttered, "You are death on a guy's ego sometimes."

A self-conscious giggle slid out of her. "What adjective would make you feel better about yourself, cowboy?"

"Hmm. Let me think." He propped his hands on his hips, his eyes glinting wickedly. "How about happy? Tell me you're happy to see me."

"I am." She didn't have to think twice about that. "You know I am." She frowned slightly, finding it hard to believe he needed any reassurance in that direction.

"Better." His voice grew lower and huskier as he stepped closer to her shoulder. "I like what you have going on in this sketch."

"Thanks. I think it has potential." She tried not to read too much into how close he was standing to her or the way his breath moved the hair against the side of her neck.

"It has more than potential," he protested quietly. "You're a master designer. That's why your family's products fly off the shelves and practically sell themselves."

She flushed in appreciation. "For a guy who spills coffee as freely as you do—"

"Ouch!"

She ignored his interruption. "You sure know how to say nice things to me."

"Double ouch! There's that word again. Nice," he repeated it in a disgusted voice.

Chuckling, she swiveled her head his way to deliver a comeback and found her face only a couple of inches away from his.

He glanced furtively around them before rasping, "Have you done any more thinking about our first kiss?"

"Ames," she gasped.

"It's a simple yes or no question." Though his voice was teasing, the look in his eyes was intense.

"Hey there, cowboy!" Lucy moved their way, interrupting the moment they'd been having.

Laura didn't know whether to be irritated or relieved. Maybe she was both. "Do you need something, Luce?" She stared at her pointedly, wondering if she'd interrupted them on purpose.

Lucy shook her head happily. "Not at all. Just had to come to say howdy to my favorite cowboy."

Ames' eyebrows rose. "Don't let Flint hear you say that. He considers himself the star of the Carson brothers' indoor rodeo show."

Laura watched them banter from beneath her lashes, wondering if her younger sister was crushing on Ames or something. A spurt of jealously came out of nowhere, leaving a bitter taste in her mouth. *Surely not!* Her sister wouldn't keep something like that from her. Would she?

"So, uh…" Ames' expression changed as he took a step away from Laura. "I'm not sure how to break this to you guys. Maybe I'm mistaken, but," he shook his head, "I ran into Brex Morrison at the Sweetheart Spectacular this morning, and he's displaying a set of nutcrackers that bear a lot of similarities to your nutcrackers."

"Brex? Selling nutcrackers?" Lucy stared at him as if she hadn't heard right. "Pretty sure he'd rather sell toys to kids that they can use to injure their eyes with or dismember bugs. That sort of thing."

"Snowmen nutcrackers, to be more precise." Ames scowled at the memory. "With custom accessories that the buyer can pick out on the spot. One of them was a small rabbit that looked like an exact replica of—" Whatever he saw on Laura's face made him stop in mid-sentence.

She felt the color drain from her face. "No," she whispered, unable to stop the piece of charcoal from slipping from her grasp. All this time she'd been wondering where her sketches for the snowmen had disappeared to. She'd intended for them to be the next rendition of nutcrackers her family produced. Though she remembered showing the proprietary drawings to Brex, the man she'd been about to marry at the time, she couldn't remember much after that. He'd broken up with her the same day.

"No," she whispered again, swaying on her stool. It was too much. Too awful, even for Brex. This was more than him borrowing the heirloom side of their branding. This was outright theft on his part!

Ames's hands gripped her upper arms, steadying her. "Breathe, Laura."

She clawed at her throat, unable to get her airways to open. It felt like they were collapsing.

"It's happening again," Lucy whimpered. "Do something, Ames!"

"Look at me, Laura," he commanded. Though he remained calm, his voice was firm.

She frantically darted her gaze over his features.

"We're going to breathe together on the count of three, alright? One. Two. Three. Breathe in." His blue gaze bored into hers, imploring her to follow his lead.

She watched him fill his lungs with air, feeling dizzy.

"Together, Laura." He gently shook her shoulders to keep her attention on him. "We're in this together, you hear?"

She nodded, growing more lightheaded by the second.

"On the count of three. One. Two. Three. Breathe in," he repeated.

This time, she was able to drag a little air into her lungs. It was more of a choking gasp, but it was air flowing in the right direction.

"Now out." He slowly released his breath.

She panted hers out in one fell swoop.

"Again, darling." His expression softened a fraction. "Breathe in."

Darling. There was something about the tender way he said the word that told her he meant it. Brex had broken her heart, betrayed her, and stolen from her. But Ames was still here. He'd promised that he'd always be here, that he'd always have her back. And at this very moment, he also had her next breath.

She spent the next minute or two just breathing in conjunction with him. When she could finally speak again, she said the most burning two words on her heart. "Thank you."

"You're welcome. That's what friends are for." There was a world of relief in his voice. His shoulders slumped a fraction, telling her he'd been more worried on her behalf that he'd been letting on.

"Should I call an ambulance?" Lucy sounded close to tears as she bent to pick up the piece of charcoal her sister had dropped.

"Nah, it's just a dumb panic attack." Ames rubbed his thumbs in slow circles over her upper arms. "Laura's stronger than she looks. She's got it under control."

She leaned into his touch. He stepped closer, allowing her to slump at long last against his rock solid chest. She closed her eyes, feeling as safe and as cherished as a stray kitten in the arms of a fireman.

Ames didn't try to fill the silence. He simply held her, rubbing one large hand in a slow circle across her back.

"You're right," she finally confessed in a small voice. "The snowmen were my design. I misplaced them before I had a chance to show them to Lucy or our parents. At least, I thought I'd misplaced them. Now I know the truth."

"You mean he stole them from you?" Lucy sounded like she was gnashing her teeth.

"I don't know." Laura truly didn't know how they'd ultimately ended up in his hands. "I showed them to him. That's all I can tell you. After he broke up with me, I couldn't find them. I was in such a bad headspace after that, I sort of forgot all about them. Until now."

"We can't let him get away with this," Lucy seethed. "There has to be something we can do."

"There most certainly is." Ames sounded grim. "We can report him to the vendor oversight committee and get him booted from the craft fair."

"No." Laura straightened on her stool. "Let me handle this."

Ames' hand slid away from her back.

Lucy stared at her, aghast. "How?"

"I'm going to confront him." She wanted the truth, and this might be the only way she was ever going to get it.

"Not alone you're not," her sister snapped.

Laura sought out Ames' gaze again. "Do you feel up to doing a little more pickup riding?"

"For you?" He cocked his head at her. "Always."

His words filled her with warmth, chasing away some of the coldness created by his latest revelation about Brex.

❄

It was with a heavy heart that Laura explained to her parents where she was going and what she was going to do when she got there.

Haruki Lee's mouth tightened with disapproval. "I'll go with you." He laid down the carving tool he'd been wielding.

"Ames has already offered to," she assured quickly.

Her father speared him with dark, angry eyes. Then he slowly nodded. "Go."

Ames drove her in silence the short distance to the Pinetop Civic Center. He didn't speak until he found a parking spot. Then he turned to her, looking resigned. "You ready for this?"

She nodded, though it was hardly the truth. How was a person supposed to prepare for a confrontation with their ex, in which they planned to accuse them of theft? There was no precedent for a situation like this. It felt like she was living out her worst nightmare all over again.

Ames opened the door and exited the truck, reaching up to give her a hand down. She refused to let his hand go, keeping a tight grip on it as they strolled toward the sandstone building.

A red and white balloon arch marked the entrance doors. Classic love songs lilted out of the speakers mounted on both sides of them.

Only when Ames held open the door on the right for her did she drop his hand. Pinetop was a small town where people needed little provocation to start rumors about who was dating who. She was in no mood to feed that beast. She was a woman on a mission — to get some answers at long last.

As she and Ames approached Brex's booth together, he slowed his steps. "Since you asked for a pickup rider, I reckon that means you want me to hold back for now?"

"I think that would be best." She gave him a beseeching look. "Just don't go far. Please?"

For an answer, he pressed a hand to his heart.

"Thank you." She clung to his gaze for an extended moment. Then she reluctantly let it go.

It felt like one of the longest, hardest walks of her life to finish the last twenty to thirty steps toward Brex's craft booth. She walked right up to the table and stared pointedly at him, waiting for him to notice her presence.

He was speaking with a customer, accepting payment for one of his snowmen nutcrackers.

It gave her time to get an eyeful of the snowmen. Her heart sank a little further with each detail she took in. There was no denying it. As she'd feared, Brex had stolen her designs.

She could sense the moment he noticed her. The professional smile he had pasted on faded as he finished the transaction and faced her.

"I can explain." It was three short words, but they were as good as an admission of guilt.

"Please do." Her voice shook.

"This." He eloquently spread his hands to take in the wide table weighed down with snowmen. "This is the real reason I came to Pinetop."

"To make money off a set of stolen designs?" Her voice was brittle. "*My* designs?"

His expression seemed to crumble. "Of course not! Don't you get it?" His voice grew hoarse with urgency. "I wanted to help bring one of your dreams to life. To show you what could've been if I hadn't given up on us. To show you what we can still have together if you're willing to give us another chance."

She was momentarily rendered speechless. The last thing she'd expected was for him to admit outright what he'd done, much less turn it into some twisted attempt at proving he'd done it for her.

"I'm not ready to give up on us, Laura." His voice grew silky soft.

"But you did." She finally found her voice. "That's exactly what you did. You've betrayed my trust on so many levels. This isn't right." She waved her hands at the snowmen nutcrackers. "You did this without my permission, and you're making money off of it."

His mouth twisted bitterly. "So that's it, huh? You're gonna just report me and get me kicked out of town?"

"I didn't say that." She lifted her chin. "I think I have a right to know what you're doing with the money."

He blew out a gusty breath. "Listen. If you want a cut—"

"I said I want to know what you're doing with the money," she snapped.

"What do you think?" His expression grew shuttered. "I'm sending it to the nursing home in Nevada like I always do. Got both of my grandparents there now."

And now we're back into morally gray territory. Were there no depths the man wouldn't stoop to? Even so, she couldn't bear the thought of pulling the plug on his sales cold turkey and indirectly getting his grandparents pitched out of their nursing home into the street.

"How about you consider the snowmen my donation to charity?" Her voice grew chilly. "But if you ever again take something from me without my permission, I'm going to the police."

A matching brand of frigidness glinted in his eyes. Then he ducked his head, effectively hiding it from view. "You still care. This proves it."

"All it proves is that I've had to forgive you twice." Her words dropped like ice cubes between them.

"I still care." He yanked his head up to meet her gaze. The coldness had disappeared. "How could I not? You're the kindest, most beautiful person I've ever met." His voice grew pleading.

Yet you were awfully quick to let me go. It was going to take a lot more than a few rapid-fire apologies and cheap compliments to convince her that he'd changed. So far, she hadn't seen any evidence of that. On the contrary, she was finding out things she'd never known about him, things that were starting to make her wonder if she'd ever truly known him in the first place.

❄

It was no fun facing her sister and parents following her decision not to press charges against Brex.

"You mean you're just going to let him off the hook?" Lucy looked ready to explode.

Ames' gaze narrowed on hers. "What about the oversight committee? Even if you don't press charges, they could at least boot him from the craft fair and make him ineligible to participate in any future ones around Pinetop."

She shook her head. "Considering what he's using the money for..." It was difficult to explain, but she tried. "I get that what he's doing is wrong, but I wouldn't be able to live with myself if I had any part in his failure to continue making payments to his grandparents' nursing home."

"Yes, it's wrong!" Lucy threw her hands into the air. "On so many levels that I don't even know where to begin!"

"She's right." Ames' sad expression almost did Laura in. It was one thing for him to be irritated by Brex's dishonesty. It was another thing entirely for him to be disappointed in *her*.

"I'm sorry," she murmured to him as she walked him to his truck. "For the first time since we've met, I don't think I want to know what you think about me right now." Nothing good, that was for sure.

"Probably not." He snorted as he bowed his head over his door handle. "Unless you're ready for our first kiss."

She burst out laughing. "That's a little...unexpected."

He lifted his head to meet her gaze. "Why?"

She waved a hand helplessly. "How could you possibly be thinking about kissing me at a time like this?"

He looked surprised by the question. "Because I'm always thinking about kissing you."

He pulled open the door and climbed behind the wheel, shutting the door firmly behind him. Revving the motor, he waved two fingers at her through the window and roared off.

CHAPTER 6: WHAT IS

Saturday

Ames often dropped by the toy store to bring Laura a shot of her favorite espresso on his way to Castellano's. This morning, however, he texted to say he was heading straight to work today. He and his brothers were putting in some extra hours of practice before tonight's rodeo performance, and he wanted to get an early start.

Unaccountable disappointment flooded her. Though he was under no obligation to bring her coffee, it felt like he was avoiding her. A few minutes later, a driver in a Gingerbread House uniform stepped into the store. He was holding a cardboard box, bearing two tall, familiar-looking cups. A swirl of steam rose from each of them.

"Morning," he called cheerfully, glancing around the store. "I have a special delivery of espresso for a Miss Laura Lee and Miss Lucy Lee."

Laura shyly raised her hand. "I'm Laura."

"And I'm Lucy." Lucy breezed up to the guy with an armful of wooden blocks to greedily claim her cup. "Wow!"

She spun delightedly in her sister's direction. "Ames is upping his game, huh?" She'd just finished disinfecting the armful of blocks in the back, and she was returning them to the children's play zone. It was a gated off area in a corner of the room, paved with rubber mats in primary colors. This was the place where children could test out toys before their parents purchased them — blocks, rocking horses, dollhouses, and more. It was the most popular spot in the store, and it resulted in a lot of sales.

"I don't know what you're talking about." After ensuring that they didn't owe the delivery guy anything, Laura gave him an extra tip, knowing Ames had likely already done so. Then she followed her sister to help set up the play area for the day. She found herself smiling for no reason at all. Ames just had that effect on her. The sweet stuff he was forever doing for her never failed to put her in a better mood.

"Oh, I think you do." Lucy rolled her eyes. "So, have you kissed him yet?"

"Just stop." Feeling her face grow warm, Laura breathed in the delectable scent of espresso before taking her first sip.

"I'll take that as a no." Lucy made a face at her. "Seriously, what are you waiting for? You're into him. He's into you..." She let her voice trail off suggestively.

"Flint Carson is just as into you, and I don't see you doing anything about that, either." For weeks, Laura had been wanting to bring up the topic, but the right opportunity hadn't come along until now. Their parents were in their glassed-in workshop, and the store wouldn't open for another ten minutes, so the microphones weren't turned on yet. It was the perfect time for a sister chat.

Lucy gave her an are-you-crazy look. "Flint Carson doesn't have a serious bone in his body!"

"In his very tall, very ripped rodeo champ body, you

mean," Laura pressed in a teasing voice, watching closely for her sister's reaction.

Lucy avoided her gaze. "I'm not denying that all three Carson brothers are hunks of burning ho-ho-holy hotness. But he's got enough single ladies drooling over him. He doesn't need to add me to that Santa-sized list."

Laura could hear an underlying note of jealousy in her voice. "But he wants to." She couldn't resist pointing out that undeniable fact.

Though Lucy didn't deny it, she shrugged as if it didn't matter. "I think the only thing he finds fascinating about me is the fact that I'm not chasing after him like, every other single lady in this town. I'm a puzzle he's trying to figure out. Nothing more."

"If you say so." Laura was far from convinced that was the case.

"I do." Lucy adopted a dismissive voice that told Laura she was done talking about him. However, that didn't explain the flush staining her creamy features or the agitated way she was slapping blocks together to form a tower. Or how off kilter it was and how quickly it collapsed.

Laura took another sip of her coffee before sliding to her knees to help out. "Somebody's off their game this morning. I hope my teasing about Flint isn't what did the trick." To drive her point home, she constructed a straighter tower that stood twice as tall as Lucy's next one. It wasn't half bad, actually. She rocked back a little to admire it.

Lucy zinged a block in her direction, sending it toppling to the floor. "Oops!" There was scant apology ringing in her tone. "Guess you're right about me being off my game."

Laura rolled her eyes and abandoned her mission to help get the play zone ready for the day. "Clearly, you don't need my help here."

"Clearly," Lucy chuckled. She looked a little less grumpy than before.

They were on the schedule to take their lunch breaks in pairs today. That way they could attend the grand opening festivities of the newest shop in town, a jewelry store called All That Glitters. Their parents took the first lunch break at the crack of noon and returned with a shiny new gold bracelet on her mother's wrist, one made of fourteen-karat gold beads in the shape of cats. She'd won it in some opening day drawing. Talk about luck!

"I love it!" Laura oohed and aahed over it while Lucy finished helping a customer. "I've always wanted a cat," she reminded, nudging her mother suggestively with her elbow. "Now that we're no longer traveling the country in a teensy tiny travel trailer, we should consider getting a pet."

Her father grunted. "The poor critter would be home alone all day long. What kind of life is that?"

Laura pursed her lips thoughtfully. "Maybe we could bring him to the shop?" she suggested hopefully.

Her mother was shaking her head before she finished the question. "Too many people are allergic to cats, I'm afraid."

"What if you and Dad kept him in the workshop with you?" There had to be a way to make it work. People adopted pets all the time. People who were busy. People who worked the same long hours she and her family did.

Lucy waited until they were on their lunch break at one o'clock to offer her input into the topic of adoption. "I can put a bug in Ames' ear for you about that cat you want so bad. I betcha he'll find a way to get you one. Or three. Or fifty. Maybe he and Flint would be willing to raise a whole herd of felines for you in their bachelor pad next door."

Laura smiled, wondering if it was true. It certainly sounded like something Ames would do, but it wouldn't be fair to pressure him into handling the care and upkeep of a pet for her. That would be taking advantage of his kindness... and the very serious crush he seemed to have on her. Just thinking about it made her heart do a crazy flip-flop. Okay, a whole series of flip-flops, followed by a few cartwheels, and a triple backflip.

She glanced away to hide the butterflies fluttering inside her stomach. "He and his brothers are gone as much as we are. I doubt they're in any more of a position to adopt a pet."

"Don't know until you ask," Lucy noted impishly.

"Please don't." Laura's voice grew thready. She really, really, really didn't want to put that kind of pressure on Ames right now. Their relationship was already experiencing enough growing pains.

Giving her an odd look, her sister finally dropped the topic. For now. Or maybe she fell silent because they'd reached the grand opening of Pinetop's newest boutique. A throng of people surrounded the entrance to the jewelry store.

Laura and Lucy exchanged a wry glance, both silently acknowledging that it would take longer than their one-hour lunch break to make it inside the store. There was a pretty lengthy line waiting to get in.

Lucy stepped closer to Laura to murmur, "Guess that's what happens when you give away a free gold bracelet."

Or more than one. According to the excited chatter around them, a drawing for a second gold bracelet was about to take place soon.

"Maybe I'm just a simple elf," Laura joked, backing away from the growing army of spectators, "but I don't need or want a gold bracelet badly enough to risk being trampled." The tiny local news station had two cameramen on site, filming the event with cameras elevated on poles.

A child, who was stuck in line between two adults holding her hands, suddenly squealed. She tried to wiggle from their grasp and managed to break one hand free. She pointed frenziedly at Laura and Lucy. "Look, Mom! Elves! Real ones." She couldn't be more than four or five-years-old.

Laura felt sorry for the child, knowing she would be having a lot more fun at Santa's Toy Factory. Instead, she was shivering outside in the mountain breeze with parents who probably weren't going to win the next gold bracelet.

She and Lucy curtsied in their elf skirts and candy cane striped stockings, blowing kisses at the little girl. She started to jump up and down, begging to have her picture taken with the elves.

The sisters ended up posing with her and several more children. The parents thanked them profusely for helping break the monotony of standing in line. One even offered them a tip, which Laura quickly refused. Instead, she took the opportunity to invite them to pay a visit to the toy store later on.

"When you're done being a walking advertisement..." Lucy tugged on her arm to get her moving again. "Our lunch break isn't going to last forever. Our best bet, at this point, is grabbing lunch at our favorite sandwich truck on the way back."

"It's a date!" Laura momentarily paused in front of the All That Glitters display windows. Like nearly every other shop in town, the store windows were drenched in Christmas lights. Theirs were all white with gold foil accents, an entrancing mix of holiday spirit and glam that was well suited to a jewelry store.

"You seriously can't resist shiny things." Lucy quit tugging on her arm and joined her at the window, pointing at one of the pieces of jewelry on display. "There's your ring, sis!"

Laura followed her finger, surprised to see a massive square diamond on a simple white gold band. "That's at least five karats!" She couldn't imagine spending that kind of money on a ring. Ever.

"I know, and it's exactly the kind of ring Ames is gonna spring for when the time comes. Mark my words." Lucy batted her lashes teasingly.

"Luce," Laura groaned. "You really don't have to say everything that pops into your head." Her younger sister had been born without a filter. It was no wonder Flint was so into her. They had that unfortunate trait in common.

"Whatever." Lucy rolled her eyes. "I was just pointing out the obvious."

"Are you?" Laura gave her a warning head shake. "What part of *we're not dating* can't you seem to get through your noggin?" She was still too messed up in the head over her breakup with Brex to give another relationship a fair shot at the moment. *Sorry, Ames!* She truly was, but he deserved better than a bunch of rebound nonsense. It was such a shame that Brex had popped into town when he did. She'd just about reached the point of being able to move on with her life. Then he'd shown his arrogant mug and ripped off the scab again.

"Uh...maybe because a certain crazy good looking bronc rider kisses you with his eyes every time he sees you." Lucy employed her duh voice, like she was trying to communicate with someone who was really dense.

He does? Laura stared at her, perplexed. Was it really that obvious to others?

Lucy wasn't looking her way. She was pointing to another ring. "Now *that's* more my style." It was a marquise diamond set in a diamond-encrusted sterling silver band.

"It looks like something that belongs in a museum," Laura sighed, leaning closer to get a better look at the intricate details etched into the side of the band. "It's absolutely stunning." It was a one-of-a-kind ring, the work of a master designer.

"I know. Utterly perfect for this go-big-or-go-home kind of gal." Lucy wiggled the fingers on her left hand with a faraway look, clearly envisioning it on her ring finger.

It was Laura's turn to bat her eyelashes. "I'll be sure to let Flint know."

"You do that." Lucy snorted, sounding more amused than worried as she swung away from the window. "Tell him if he buys me a ring that nice, I might have to consider dating his cocky self, after all."

Laura burst out laughing. Her sister joined in. They strolled arm in arm down the street together, stopping at their favorite truck vendor to purchase grilled jerk chicken sandwiches. The brioche buns were filled to overflowing with pineapple slices, coleslaw, and shredded chicken.

"Pinetop serves the best food on the planet," Lucy declared between bites. "I'm practically inhaling this thing."

Laura was amused by the way her words became muffled by her next gigantic bite. "You must have worked up an appetite rebuilding my block tower after accidentally knocking it down earlier."

"Holding grudges, are we?" Lucy munched her way with gusto through the delectable sandwich as they strolled back to the toy store.

A loud mechanical wail shrilly rode the breeze, making them slow their steps.

Lucy abruptly swallowed the bite she'd been chewing. "Is that a security alarm?"

"I think so." Laura turned to scan the row of holiday boutiques on both sides of the street behind them. "Hopefully, it's just a test." Or maybe someone had burned a bag of popcorn and set off a smoke detector. She doubted it was much more than that. This was Pinetop, a peaceful little town whose crime rate had to be down near zero.

The shriek of a police siren joined the melee, verifying that what they were hearing was not, in fact, some sort of security alarm test. Lights flashed, uniformed officers ushered the crowd back, and police tape was rolled out in front of one of the shops.

"It's the jewelry store!" Lucy craned her neck for a closer look, but the number of spectators standing between them and the store quickly swelled. It was difficult to make out much of what was happening.

"Nothing we can do," Lucy muttered, half turning away. "Let's get out of here."

Laura agreed. And though she was dying to know what was going on, she knew the best thing they could do right now was stay out of law enforcement's way. It wasn't like they'd been close enough to witness anything useful. It was with a heavy heart that she returned with her sister to the toy store.

Their mother, who'd been covering the showroom floor while they were away, gave them a sweeping look of concern. "Why the long faces?" She was wearing a Mrs. Santa outfit today, complete with a white wig and silver spectacles that her sharp eyes didn't require for reading. Her Asian features gave the outfit an exotic twist that rarely failed to make her girls smile.

However, Laura couldn't have felt less like smiling. Sadness tightened her insides as she shared the unfortunate news. "It appears that All That Glitters was robbed."

Her mother yanked off her spectacles. "But you were just there! So were we! How in the—?"

"I don't know," Laura shook her head. "We never made it inside. They were wall to wall with people, and there was a huge line snaking down the sidewalk. It would've taken hours to get through it."

"Are you sure it was the jewelry store?" Ayaka Lee worriedly twisted the new bracelet around her wrist.

"Very sure," Lucy declared flatly.

"On their opening day, no less," their mother sighed. "What a shame!"

Laura nodded, wishing she knew more. In the entire year she and her family had lived in Pinetop, she couldn't recall hearing anything about a store being robbed. Or any shoplifting being reported. Or vandalism. The worst thing she'd witnessed before today was a deputy issuing a citation to a driver who'd blatantly run a stoplight.

The jewelry store robbery felt new and sinister, like things around them were changing and not in a good way. She wasn't the only one who felt that way. Word quickly spread around Pinetop about the shocking theft that had taken place in broad daylight. Cell phone video clips of the incident flooded social media.

According to the news anchors, nobody the sheriff and his deputies interviewed was a hundred percent sure what had happened, not even the patrons who'd been standing inside the jewelry boutique. One second, the place had been filled with happy, chatting customers. The next second, the security alarm had gone off. Nobody recalled seeing who broke the glass on the display case in question, and nobody remembered seeing anyone reach through the broken glass to steal anything.

More than a dozen diamond rings had simply vanished. A special bulletin was released to the public, announcing that the store owners were turning over their security tapes to the police. Laura could sense that the citizens of Pinetop were taking a collective breath and holding it. She did the same, anxiously keeping an eye on the news updates on her phone app for the rest of the afternoon.

Lord willing, what was recorded on the footage would lead to an arrest.

❄

Sheriff Dean Skelton paced his office as five o'clock approached. His lips moved in silent prayer for a report back from the forensics experts he'd reached out to. Since it was a Friday afternoon, he knew the chances were slim he'd hear anything before the close of business today. However, he'd implored them to put a rush on it, assuring them he'd pay extra for a same-day turnaround. He'd take any news at all at this point.

Nothing like this had ever happened in Pinetop before. Naturally, the mayor was clamoring for an answer. So were the local news anchors and everyone else. Something like this could really damage the family friendly atmosphere the citizens had worked so hard to build. Safe streets, homes, and businesses were an integral part of what attracted vacationers to come shop in their small-town boutiques instead of spending their hard-earned money in bigger cities.

I need to get to the bottom of this, and soon.

The phone on the sheriff's desk lit up with an incoming call. It was the forensics office. Drawing a deep breath, he took a seat in his swivel chair and reached for the receiver, knowing he probably wasn't going to like what they had to tell him.

He didn't.

Apparently, both security cameras had been pushed far enough to the side so that neither had recorded who or what had shattered the display case. It wasn't a simple setup error on the security company's part, either. Or a coincidence. Someone had tampered with the cameras.

A carefully coordinated kind of tampering, as it turned out. The video feeds of both cameras shifted to other parts of the boutique in one well-synchronized movement. It happened so quickly that only a stick-like blur had been captured by the video feeds. The forensic team's working theory was that retractable wands had been employed in the diversion.

From the loud cheering in the background of the clip, it was additionally determined that the thieves had made their move right after the announcement of a winner to the jewelry store's second giveaway. One happy woman could be seen joyously clasping on another one of All That Glitter's custom gold bracelets.

While the video cameras recorded the cheering and clapping of the onlookers, the owners of the jewelry store had simultaneously suffered a loss of nearly a hundred thousand dollars in stolen gems.

It was a puzzle that was going to take some good old-fashioned detective work to solve. It was going to take time. It wasn't going to happen tonight.

Dean Skelton thanked the forensics experts for their assistance. Grimacing, he dialed the mayor next.

❄

Though it was closing time, the shop owners on Main Street lingered in their doorways and on the sidewalks outside, wearing troubled expressions as they tried to come to grips with what had happened.

Laura and her parents couldn't help overhearing some of their conversations as they locked the front doors of Santa's

Toy Factory. Lucy had pulled the Jeep around front and was waiting for them at the curb with the motor idling.

One boutique owner gave a soulful sigh. "It sure won't look the same with bars on all the shop windows in town."

"Let's hope it doesn't come to that," another woman soothed. "Lots for us to pray about, that's for sure."

The drive home was punctuated by somber silence. Each of them was lost in their own thoughts.

Laura waited until Lucy pulled into their lower-level garage before announcing, "I think I'm going to head to Castellano's this evening." After Ames' one and only text this morning, she hadn't heard anything else from him, not even a response to her thank you text for the espresso he'd had delivered to her and Lucy. His silence felt out of character. Maybe she was reading too much into things. Maybe she was simply allowing the unfortunate events at the jewelry store to affect her mood. Regardless, she wanted to go see for herself that things were still okay between her and Ames.

"I'll go with you," Lucy offered.

"Please do." Their father gave a decided nod as he climbed out of the Jeep. "It would be safest to stick together after everything that's happened today."

"I agree." Their mother reached for the hand he was holding out to her to assist her from the Jeep. She continued clinging to his hand as they made their way up the stairs to start dinner.

"Mom, we'll wait and eat at Castellano's," Laura called after them. There was no point in eating before heading to a dinner theater.

"Enjoy yourselves," Ayaka Lee called back, sounding a little more cheerful. She and her husband loved piddling in the kitchen together. They were forever stirring up dishes from their childhood days in Japan — katsu chicken, sushi rolls, and crab rice with edamame.

Lucy took her time strapping her crossbody purse around her and reaching back inside the Jeep to retrieve her insulated coffee mug from the console. It wasn't until the door shut behind their parents that she asked, "Why the sudden need to pay a visit to Castellano's?"

Laura shrugged, not sure how to voice her latest string of uncertainties. "I just want to make sure Ames is okay."

Lucy fiddled with the strap on her purse. "Why wouldn't he be?"

"I don't know." Laura really hoped she was imagining the pulling away vibes she was getting from him. "He's been really quiet today."

"He had your favorite coffee delivered," her sister reminded, pushing the button on the wall panel to shut the garage door.

"I know, but he hasn't responded to my thank you for it, and that was hours ago." Because of the robbery, it felt like days ago. Laura met her sister's questioning gaze, wondering if she even had the right to be worried. She'd made it painfully clear that she and Ames were just friends. To him. To her sister. To everyone.

Lucy studied her soberly. "Can I say something without getting my head bitten off?"

Laura's lips parted in surprise. "You mean you finally found a filter?" What was the world coming to?

Lucy rolled her eyes. "I'll take that as a yes. Listen." She grimaced and seemed to be searching for the right words. "I know Brex hurt you in ways I may never understand, but that's not Ames' fault. And you've been stringing that poor cowboy along for months and months and months."

"No!" Laura's agonized protest filled the garage. "There was no stringing. I didn't even realize he felt that way until—" She bit her lip, wishing she hadn't said so much.

Her sister didn't hesitate to pounce on the revelation. "So

you two *have* talked about getting together," she crowed in an aha voice.

"He wants to," Laura admitted. "I, um...sort of just found out he's been feeling that way for a while."

Lucy shook her head in disgust. "And they say guys are dumb!"

"I know. It's just all happening so fast, and now Brex is in town, and I'm a wreck all over again." Laura blinked rapidly to hold back the sting of tears. "It wouldn't be fair to Ames to try to get something going with him right now."

Lucy snorted. "Somehow, I don't think the timing would matter to him. He's got it for you so bad I almost feel sorry for him." She spun in Laura's direction. "If we leave right now, you can probably catch him before the show."

"In our elf costumes?" Laura stared in dismay down at her red felt dress and the upturned toes of her elf boots.

Lucy gaped at her. "I'm not even going to grace that question with a response." She stomped toward the stairs.

Right. Laura hurried after her for a lightning shower and a change of clothing. Instead of jeans, she selected a corduroy dress of blue velvet that fell just above her knees. She paired it with soft suede boots in a light beige color. They hugged her legs, adding a much needed layer of warmth to the February temps. Since the two of them wouldn't be outside for long, she opted to leave her winter coat at home.

"That should get his attention." Lucy cast an approving sideways look at her on their way back to the Jeep. She mashed the button on the wall to open the garage door.

The cold mountain air immediately swirled into the garage, making Laura shiver.

"You think?" She smoothed her hands nervously over the skirt of her dress as she clasped her seatbelt and settled into the passenger seat.

"If you don't want to take my word for it, wait and see

what Ames has to say about it," her sister advised cheekily. She started the motor.

❄

Laura found Ames in the lower-level stables, brushing down the horse he'd be riding that evening. At the sight of her, he shoved the brush at his youngest brother and strode her way up the long, plank hallway. Horses nickered from the stalls on both sides of him.

"What are you doing here?" His blue gaze darkened as he drank her in.

She felt like a flower blossoming in the sun beneath the intensity of his scrutiny. A guy like him didn't need to fill the air between them with words. All it took was one look from him to make her feel special. Cherished. Adored. Wanted.

She smiled at the sound his leather chaps made as his long legs ate up the stretch of hallway between them.

"I came to see you."

The admiring glow in his gaze was immediately replaced with concern. "Is everything okay?"

"Yes and no." She was full of too many conflicting emotions to put a label on what she was feeling.

He reached for her shoulders and spun her around to face the opposite direction. "We can talk in the Carsons' home away from home, if you prefer."

He and his brothers had a dressing room all to themselves. She'd only been inside it one other time.

Her heart beat an insane rhythm as he led her to it. Shutting the door behind them, he leaned back against it and faced her. "What'll it be this time, darling? More pickup rider services?"

"No." She forced herself to swallow her pride and take a step closer, resting a hand on his arm. The sleeves of his plaid shirt were rolled up. She stifled a shiver at the way his muscles flexed beneath her fingers. "I, um…" Oh, this was so much harder than she'd anticipated! She suddenly wished she'd taken the time to rehearse what she was going to say.

Ames watched her with a hooded expression. "You sure you're okay?"

"I'm trying to be, but I've been worried about you." The words burst from her.

"Worried about me?" He pointed at his chest, looking puzzled. "Why?"

She glanced away from him, blinking nervously. "I know this may sound stupid, but you didn't respond to my thank you text for the coffee. Then the jewelry store was broken into. Lucy and I had just left—"

"You were there?" Ames straightened against the door, reaching for her hands.

"We didn't go inside." She shook her head. "We tried dropping by their grand opening celebration during our lunch break, but it was too crowded to get through the door. On our way back to the toy store, we heard the security alarm go off." If he'd been watching or listening to the news, he already knew the rest of the story.

"Did you see anything?" He rubbed his callused thumbs in circles over the tops of her hands.

"No. There were way too many people between us and the store."

"Good." He tugged her closer so he could rest his chin on top of her head. "That's messy business. I'm glad you're not involved."

"So we're okay?" She snuggled closer, reveling in his nearness and scent — a mix of saddle soap, leather, and the faint overtones of aftershave. "You and me?"

He grew still. "Any reason we shouldn't be?"

She felt silly reminding him, but she didn't know what else to say. "You still haven't responded to my text."

"Ah." He hugged her tighter. "Figured I'd leave you alone for a while. You know...give you some space. Flint said I follow you around like a needy puppy, and girls find that annoying."

Nothing could've been further from the truth in his case. "I don't find you annoying," she assured fervently.

"Good to know." One large hand threaded through her hair, cupping the back of her head. "You gonna get around to telling me what's wrong before the show starts?"

She nodded against his shirt. "Lucy said I've been stringing you along. Is that what you think I've been doing?" Her shoulders shook from the effort to hold back a sob.

"What? No!" He leaned back a little to scowl down at her. "Lucy's wrong, you hear?"

She nodded, unable to keep her eyes from filling.

"What you and I have is special," he continued in a gruff voice. "It doesn't need to fit any mold. It's ours."

She fisted her hands in his shirt. "I just needed you to hear it from me...that I would never, ever, ever knowingly do anything to hurt you, Ames. You mean too much to me. I've just been so caught up in my—"

"I know," he interrupted. "It's okay." He let her go, but only long enough to reach for her face and cup it gently between his hands. "You and I are okay. Promise."

"Are we?" She felt herself crumpling from the inside out. "Now that I know the truth about how you feel about me, I feel so selfish."

"Well, don't." He cast a reluctant glance at the clock hanging on the wall behind her. "Listen, I don't have much longer before I have to be in the ring, but I'm gonna let you in on a little secret."

She searched his rugged features, needing to see for

herself that he was okay with the way things stood between them.

He ducked his head over hers, blocking out everything but the sincerity in his voice and expression. "The way you've grieved over your broken engagement tells me that commitments like that mean something to you. You don't toss your affections around lightly. From my angle, the next guy who manages to get a ring on your finger will be the most fortunate guy on the planet."

She swayed closer to him, feeling like she was floating on clouds and rainbows. "If you still want that kiss you've been gunning for," she murmured, "take it. I'm ready."

"No. You're not." He brushed his thumbs beneath her eyes, wiping away the dampness. "You'll know when you are, and so will I."

"Ames," she sighed as he dropped his arms and reached for the door handle. A fresh wave of anxiety rose in her throat.

"Laura," he echoed, treating her to a very thorough once over. He spent their last moments together raking her longingly with his gaze from head to toe, assuring in a way that no words could've ever done that the dress she'd chosen to wear this evening was a roaring success.

"Relax, darling. I'll text you back." Humor twinkled in his gaze as he pulled open the door.

It was just the right thing to say to her to ease her remaining fears, and he probably knew it.

A damp chuckle pealed out of her. "I'll be the one cheering the loudest for you out there tonight."

"You'd better be." He kissed her again with his eyes. Then he was gone.

CHAPTER 7: DISAPPEARING ACT

Mid March

Before Ames exited the tiny hangar that housed the pair of crop dusters shared by the ranchers in Pinetop, he could already sense the small mountain town was abuzz with something new. Posters were on display everywhere, including the wall he parked their Canyon Creek Ranch jet beside. It was advertising something called the Spring Awakening Gala. From the pictures, it looked like they were talking about a parade, one that would mark the official start of springtime.

Yep. Only in Pinetop!

You could be gone a few days and miss a landmark annual celebration. It was kind of hilarious how the locals made such a big deal out of, well, everything. As much as he and his brothers joked about it, he was going to miss it when they moved back home.

They'd stalled on making that decision for just about as long as they could for one very big, very monumental reason — Pinetop had changed their lives. A part of their hearts would always belong to this small mountain town. Ames anticipated many return visits back. Regular ones. There was a good chance they'd continue to perform at Castellano's, just a few weeks here and there. They were still negotiating the details about that.

It would've never worked. None of this going back and forth between Dallas and Pinetop would've ever worked without Ames' pilot's license. Nor would it have worked without one of the top foremen in the west helping run their horse ranch during their absence, a highly experienced foreman who'd just last night turned in his three-month notice. Come summer, he was heading overseas to accept a job at a much larger horse ranch in England.

Ames had yet to break the news to his brothers. It was going to spark a very serious conversation. One they'd been putting off for months. One that would require them to set an official end date to their extended stay in Pinctop.

Flint was waiting for him outside the hangar in the two-toned Chevy pickup they'd been sharing during their stint in Pinetop.

He waggled his eyebrows as Ames jogged up to the passenger door and yanked it open. "How was Dallas?"

Ames was pretty sure he detected a hint of homesickness in the question. "Interesting." He wasn't sure if now was the time to deliver his news.

"How so?" Flint revved the motor and started rolling forward while Ames was still getting buckled in.

Guess it's the right time, after all. "Our foreman just turned in his three-month notice." Ames dug the letter out of the back pocket of his jeans and waved the crumpled sheet of paper beneath Flint's nose.

"I should've seen that coming." Ignoring the letter Ames was holding out, Flint hunched over the steering wheel, looking sulky.

"How so?" Ames hadn't seen anything coming. He was

just grateful they had three months to figure out what they were going to do about it.

Flint shrugged. "Nothing exciting has been happening at Canyon Creek Ranch since we accepted this gig in Pinetop. Our staff there has been in a perennial holding pattern. We brought our top horse trainer with us and everything. To be honest, I'm surprised our foreman is the only one we've lost so far."

"Good point." There was no way Nash would've left Noelle behind in Dallas. She'd played too important of a role in his long road to recovery. He'd needed her at his side far more than they needed her churning out rodeo horses in Dallas.

"That's why I made it," Flint grumbled. "If we want to stay on the map as one of the top horse training ranches in the west, we're gonna have to get our boots back on the ground in Dallas. Don't get me wrong. This going back and forth has been fun, but…"

"And necessary for Nash," Ames interjected. Their oldest brother had desperately needed this transition time between the national bronc riding circuit and his retirement from the rodeo industry. It had kept his spirits from flagging as he adjusted to his new life as an amputee. Getting married along the way and having a bun in the oven was just the icing on the cake — God style.

An enormous sense of gratitude welled inside Ames' chest. He pointed upward with both forefingers. *Thank you, Lord. For bringing us through another really tough challenge.* While in Pinetop, all three brothers had grown closer to each other and to God. They were stronger now. Better men. More ready to face what came next. He was pretty sure that meant all three of them would be retiring from the rodeo circuit. It was going to be another huge transition, this time to full-time ranching.

"Agreed." Flint drove them from the outskirts of town to Main Street. "Though Nash hasn't said anything to me about it yet, I think he's getting as homesick as you and I are. It might have something to do with having a kid on the way."

"It might." Ames waved their foreman's resignation letter in the air again. "This is going to force us to make some tough decisions."

"Maybe we can have our sit down over dinner this evening." They reached the business district. Flint hung a left and set their course for Castellano's. "Since you just got back into town, they're giving us the night off. Christie Hart will be filling in with her newest trick riding routine. She's been working on two new stunts that she's ready to unveil." Though she was now married to local mechanic Wes Wakefield, she continued to go by her maiden name while in the ring. It was easier than trying to rebrand her award-winning Hart of the West performance.

Ames stifled a yawn. "I don't mind taking the evening off." It might give him time to pay a quick visit to Laura. His heart thumped harder in anticipation. He'd really missed her this time.

"Me, either." Flint gave an even noisier yawn that all but rattled the windows.

Everything's a competition with you. Ames shot him a dark look. "Not sure why you're so tired. I'm the one who flew a red-eye flight back."

"Are you kidding?" Flint curled his upper lip. "I had to pick up the slack all over the place while you were away."

Ames snorted. "Something tells me that did *not* include doing laundry, washing dishes, getting the oil changed in the truck…" He ticked the list off on his fingers.

"Been keeping an eye on your girl," Flint shot back. "That should count for something."

"More like keeping an eye on her younger sister, but okay.

I'll bite. What happened while I was gone?" Ames whipped out his cell phone and settled more comfortably in the seat so he could text Laura.

I'm back. Missed you.

She still wasn't ready to hear what he really wanted to say — that he was falling in love with her. He was so far past the friendly feelings part of their relationship that it was laughable. He didn't want to scare her off by telling her the whole truth, though. Not yet.

"Caught one of the newest wranglers at Castellano's snapping a picture of her and Lucy with his cell phone. I collared the creep and made him erase it."

"Which one?" Ames tapped his phone impatiently against his palm as he waited for Laura to respond to his text.

"Some joker by the name of Oak. I think it's short for Oakley. From what I can gather, he doesn't have much of a resume, but you know how Angel and Willa Castellano feel about taking in strays."

Ames grunted as his phone vibrated with an incoming text. It was from Laura. He eagerly read it.

Missed you, too!!! Glad you're back. Want to do lunch?

Flint shot him a disgusted look as he pulled into the rear parking lot at the dinner theater. "It's hard to have a convo with a guy who takes weeks to answer."

"Sorry." Ames typed a quick affirmative answer to Laura. *Yes! Just tell me when and where.* "Anything else you've been able to find out about this Oakley?"

"Oak," Flint corrected. "Very little other than the fact he wandered into Castellano's a few months back, looking for a job. The rest is history. Chatted up the head wrangler, and he says Oak does a decent job with the horses. Oh, and he seems to think Oak and Brex are pretty tight. Got the impression they might know each other from somewhere else."

Ames yanked his head up from his phone. "Brex Morrison?" What could some wandering rodeo hand possibly have in common with Laura's ex?

Flint gave him a strange look. "You know anyone else by that ridiculous name?"

"I reckon not." Ames mulled over what his brother had told him. "How long did you say Oak has been in town?"

"Few months." Flint shrugged. "Roman can probably give you the exact date. Why?"

"Just trying to figure out if he was around when the jewelry store was robbed."

Flint gave a long, low whistle. "Affirmative."

"I know it's a long shot, but I'm toying with a new theory." Ames couldn't prove anything yet. It was only a gut feeling at this point.

"You think Gypsy Boy was in on the robbery, eh?" Flint didn't look overly disturbed by the possibility.

"If he was, he had an accomplice. That we know." Ames had been suspicious of Brex from the beginning. He was the only guy in town with a proven track record for dishonesty. Theft, to be more precise. The jewelry robbery sure fit that picture. So did the fact that he'd managed to weasel his booth of nutcrackers into the jewelry section at the Sweetheart Spectacular. Ames wasn't sure what it ultimately had to do with the heist, but it felt connected somehow.

"Yep, the police said there had to be at least two robbers." Flint grabbed a parking spot and killed the motor. "So if Brex turns out to be one of them, are you thinking Oak was his accomplice?"

"Anything is possible. As far as I know, the sheriff's department has no solid leads yet." Ames left the truck and waited for his brother to join him as he made his way down the ramp leading to the lower-level stables.

They paused inside the entrance, and Flint jammed his thumb toward the training ring. "While you play detective,

I've got some work to do with my horse. I wanna try something new tomorrow night." He didn't elaborate before taking off down the hallway.

Ames checked his phone again, but Laura still hadn't sent him a time or place for their lunch date. Yeah, he was calling it a date, at least inside his head. He was pretty sure they were about ready to cross that line. He couldn't wait. There were several more lines he was hoping to cross after that.

Looking up, he caught sight of yet another poster for Pinetop's upcoming Spring Awakening Gala. He eyed it in bemusement. Someone had tacked it to the wall of the lower level stables at Castellano's.

Like the horses care.

"It's an interesting spot for a poster, isn't it?" Castellano's head wrangler, Roman Rios, rounded the corner and paused to stand in front of the poster with him.

"My thoughts exactly." Ames flicked the back of his hand against the poster. "The horses aren't exactly rushing to sign up for the parade."

"Yet plenty of them will end up in it, anyway." Roman had grown up at Christmas Tree Farm on the edge of town, a place staffed mostly by migrant workers, which meant he was no typical wrangler. He'd worked nearly every job in the stables at Castellano's before taking on a supervisory role there. Besides training, exercising, and caring for their livestock, he was also very much involved in the show business side of things. It was his responsibility to transport the animals to and from the ring during live performances, parading them around as needed. He occasionally assisted with the stunts, as well, particularly those performed by his wife, Hope, one of the full-time actresses on staff.

"Does that mean you've already received our marching orders for the parade?" Ames had been out of the loop for the past week while in Dallas. He knew he had some catching up to do.

"I have. The mayor is asking for no less than three floats from Castellano's to lead the parade. What I'm about to tell you next is off the record for now, so keep it to yourself." He stepped closer and lowered his voice. "The town council will be handing out a special award to Angel and Willa Castellano for their enormous contribution to our town. For all the citizens they employ and their endless philanthropy projects. They're two of the most incredible people I've ever met." There was no mistaking the reverence in his voice. He was close friends with Angel, who'd also grown up at Christmas Tree Farm.

"A well-deserved honor." Ames thought very highly of Angel — right up to his hiring of Oak, that is. "Hey, I need to ask you something. Something I'd also like to keep off the record, if you don't mind."

"Sure." Frowning slightly, Roman fell into step beside him as they made their way up the hallway toward the dressing room he shared with his brothers.

Ames waited until they were seated in a pair of leather overstuffed chairs before sharing what was bothering him. "Flint told me he had a bit of a run-in with your newest wrangler."

"Oh?" Roman sat forward, looking concerned. "Anything I need to step in and handle?"

"Nah, I think they worked it out." Ames briefly described what had happened. "I know it's not a crime to snap a picture. Flint probably overreacted, but…"

"No, he was right to say something to the guy. It was a dumb thing to do. Pretty disrespectful, if you ask me." Roman rested his elbows on his thighs and dropped his chin into his hands, looking troubled. "He does a good job with the horses. Can't deny that."

"But?" Ames prodded.

"But nobody knows much about him." Roman shook his head. "Angel hired the guy when he came looking for a job, because that's how Angel is. Ever since Oak's start date, though, I've wondered if we should've done a little more looking into his background."

Ames' interest piqued. "Why's that?"

Roman grunted. "Just a gut feeling. And the fact that he sticks to himself. Usually, the younger guys hang out together after hours, but not him. The only person in town I've seen him spend time with is an out-of-towner named Brex Morrison. Like Oak, he showed up all sudden like, and now the guy is signed up as a vendor for every craft fair between now and Christmas."

"And you see that as a problem, because...?"

Roman ducked his head. "This is going to sound bad, because I've got no proof, but the two of them showed up in town right before all the robberies began."

Ames jolted. "Robberies, as in plural?" The only one he'd heard about was one that had taken place at All That Glitters.

"Yeah." Roman grimaced. "Other than the diamond ring heist, it's mostly been petty stuff. A crystal figurine here. A collectible coin there. It's been happening all over town. The only reason I know about it is because the sheriff paid me a visit the other day to ask me some questions. I think he was hoping I could shed some light on the newcomers, as well."

"Meaning Brex and Oak?"

"Yep."

Interesting. Though Ames wasn't happy about the string of petty thefts, it was proof that he wasn't the only person in town suspicious of the gypsy vendor and his creepy wrangler friend. He was silent for a moment. "My brothers and I will be happy to keep our eyes and ears open."

"I'd appreciate that." Roman gave him a grateful look. "I'll be doing the same."

"Flint will do a better job of it than me." Ames smirked. "He was born nosy."

Roman chuckled. "He's a lot of fun to be around, isn't he?"

"A barrel of laughs," Ames agreed dryly. "Just be glad you don't live with him." His phone buzzed with an incoming message. He hoped like crazy it was from Laura.

It was.

He gave it a quick glance. *Gingerbread House. Noon.* His eyes widened at the emoji kiss she'd blown his way at the end of her text.

Wow! He felt his face turning red as he and Roman stood and faced each other.

"Get some good news?" Roman eyed the cell phone in his hand.

"A lunch date." Ames pocketed his phone, turning redder.

"She must be something special." Roman grinned at him. "Word on the street is that you Carson brothers haven't done much dating since you've been in town."

Ames' eyebrows rose. "Are you forgetting Nash married a local girl?"

"You know what I mean." Roman pointed at him, chuckling. "Lot of girls wouldn't mind getting more attention from you and Flint, but you only have eyes for the Lee sisters. Or so I've heard." His dark eyes widened at Ames' expression. "Hoh, boy! That's one rumor confirmed." He punched him lightly on the shoulder before taking off.

Laura was already seated at a table when Ames arrived at the restaurant. She excitedly waved him over.

He was grinning from ear to ear as he strode her way. She was in one of her elf costumes, though she'd ditched the pointy hat. Her dark hair tumbled around her shoulders in rich waves, framing her creamy features to perfection.

"Man, it's good to see you!" Without thinking, he dipped his head over hers. At the last minute, he stopped himself from claiming her mouth. Instead, he tangled one hand in her silky hair and gave it a playful tug as he leaned in for a hug.

"You're thinking about kissing me again." Her breathless giggle surrounded him like a warm caress as he took a seat on the stool across from her. They were at one of the bar-high tables on the outer edge of the room.

"Always." He saw no point in lying about it. "So, what's new in your life?"

She sat forward, beaming a happy smile at him. "My parents have started production on my newest toy designs. They plan to debut them at the Romance in the Air craft fair in June." She waved her hands expressively. "Weddings, babies, heirloom toys…it's a loose fit, but it'll work."

He soaked in her smile, glad to see her so happy. She deserved this. Reaching for her hand, he husked, "That's great news." To his joy, she allowed him to lace their fingers together.

Glancing shyly down at their joined hands, she murmured, "People are going to talk."

He couldn't have cared less. "Let them."

A waitress breezed their way with a pair of iced teas.

"It's raspberry infused," Laura warned, looking like she was trying not to laugh. "Which may put them in the froo-froo category."

"Probably." He reached for his glass and raised it in a toast. "To the success of my favorite toy designer."

"Thank you." She tipped her glass against his.

The slice of lemon perched on the rim of his glass got dislodged in the process and toppled into her glass.

Laughing, she took a sip. "I think it's a sign," she declared softly, raising her glass again.

He smirked. "To making lemonade together?" Life sure had dealt both of them enough lemons.

"I was going to say *to us*." She smiled as they clinked glasses together again. "But that'll work, too."

"To us. I like the sound of that." Two weeks from now, his and his brothers' current contract at Castellano's would run out. Though they were already negotiating the terms of a rodeo show for a couple of weeks this summer, the three of them were undoubtedly going to have to spend more time at Canyon Creek Ranch in the coming days. There was no way around it now that their foreman had given his notice.

He could only hope his increased absences from Pinetop wouldn't hurt the progress he'd been making lately in his relationship with Laura.

❋

The next day

Though it was a Tuesday evening, Castellano's was nearly packed. By the weekend, they expected to be sold out again. The fact that the Carson brothers continued to pull record crowds was going to make it all the more difficult to determine what came next in their careers.

For now, though, Ames needed to focus on tonight's rodeo comedy routine. The storyline involved a couple of dude ranch guests played by him and Flint. They were trying to learn how to be real cowboys under the laugh-out-loud tutelage of a salty range rider played by Nash.

He waited on the back of his bronco in the chute. It wasn't an actual rodeo. Everything they did was strictly for entertainment purposes. There were no other riders competing against him, and the strap around his horse was strictly for show. It wasn't the least bit cinched in. He'd literally taught his horse to rock and buck on command. At the end of their ride, no official score would be assessed.

He was less than thrilled to discover that the wrangler assisting him inside the chute this evening was the uncommunicative Oak. The young cowboy refused to make eye contact. The few times Ames had attempted to strike up a conversation with him, he'd mumbled a response that Ames couldn't quite make out. However, he seemed comfortable with his duties. That's all that really mattered.

Oak abruptly leaned down to fiddle with the decorative strap on the bronco Ames was seated on. "It's a little loose," he muttered, giving it a swift yank.

"What are you doing?" Ames gave him an exasperated look. "Now it's too tight." Before he could signal to the wranglers manning the gate that he needed an extra few seconds to make an adjustment, the whistle blew.

His bronco shot from the chute into the ring, rocking energetically back and forth. Ames found himself gripping the rope as tightly as he would have during an actual competition. He hadn't prompted the horse to do anything yet. The creature's current snorting and bucking were all on his own.

Not good. It dawned on Ames that he was on a genuine bronc ride tonight, brought on by the too-tight strap. Unfortunately, there were no pickup riders waiting on the sidelines to ride to his aid like there had been in the past.

I'm on my own. He managed to flick a warning look in Nash's direction, but there was no guarantee that the fictitious dude ranch owner would interpret his silent SOS in time.

The horse's movements grew more frenzied as he attempted to rock the cinch loose from his belly. Precious seconds ticked past — four, five, six…

People shot to their feet across the amphitheater, cheering Ames on. All he could do was grip the rope and hope for an opportunity to leap off and make a run for the gate.

A thunder of hooves moved in his direction. Out of the corners of his eyes, he watched his brothers converge on him from both sides. Nash reached him first, angling his mount in the same direction as the bucking bronco.

"Hop on," he shouted.

Ames didn't think. He simply acted. Moments later, he was hanging onto the back of Nash's horse, being half pulled and half dragged toward the edge of the ring. He leaped and scissored his legs at the same time and managed to land on his feet, jogging the rest of the way to the gate.

Roman was holding it open, hollering his name and shooing him to safety. Oak was nowhere in sight. Flint was right behind Ames, herding the angry and frightened bronco from the ring. The gate clanged shut behind them.

The audience erupted into even louder cheers, clapping like crazy over the lifelike performance. They'd never need to know just how real it had been.

It took all hands on deck to subdue the bronco and remove the strap. Ames rubbed the horse's neck and spoke soothingly to him until he calmed down. His reddish-brown coat was slick with sweat.

"You did good, boy!" He kept up a constant stream of praise as he led him down the ramp to the stables. Nash followed on his horse. They halted and faced each other at the bottom of the ramp.

Nash was scowling ferociously. "What happened up there?"

"Oak happened." Ames spoke through gritted teeth. "Right before I left the chute, he said something about the strap being loose. Before I realized what he was up to, he reached down and gave it a yank, cinching it way too tight. The whistle rang, and you saw the rest."

"Where is he now?" Nash swung his head around, angrily searching for the wrangler who'd put his brother in such a predicament. The young cowboy was nowhere in sight.

"It's a good thing we've ridden bucking broncos before." Ames lifted his arm to wipe the perspiration from his forehead.

"That doesn't justify what Oak did." Nash's jaw tightened. "I'll be having a sit-down with Roman over this. Angel, too."

"That won't be necessary." Roman jogged down the ramp to catch up with them. "We're gonna handle this just as soon as we locate Oak."

But their newest wrangler was no longer in the theater. He'd emptied out his work locker, and his truck was missing from the parking lot.

He was gone.

❄

Five minutes earlier

LAURA COLLAPSED IN HER SEAT AS THE CROWD ROARED around her and her sister. She could barely breathe. Something had gone terribly wrong out there in the ring. She'd never before seen Ames turn so white beneath his tan. Sure, he'd played it off like the whole bronco bucking routine was part of the show, but she knew better. His horse had never jerked around so crazily before. It was like he was possessed or something.

Lucy jumped up and down in excitement beside her. Glancing down, she finally noticed that Laura had taken a seat.

She plopped down in the seat beside Laura, shouting to be heard. "What's wrong?"

Laura shook her head, still too shaken to speak.

Frowning, Lucy angled her head like she was ready to leave. "Let's get out of here." The crowd was finally starting to quiet down a little. "Show's almost over, anyway."

Laura stood on knees that felt shaky. She whipped out her cell phone as they exited the amphitheater and shot off a text to Ames.

Are you okay?

His response came back in seconds. *I'm good. Where are you?*

She hoped that meant he had time to see her before they took off. *Heading to the Jeep. And you?*

Lucy glanced her way as they headed for the Jeep. "You chatting it up again with your not quite a boyfriend?"

Laura frowned at her phone screen. "I'm trying to figure out what happened to his horse."

Her sister gave her an incredulous look. "Ames dug in his heels and made him jump a little. It was just for show."

"No, it was more than that. Something was wrong." Laura was sure of it. Her stomach was still in knots over it. "Didn't you see the look on his face?"

"No. I was too busy watching his horse. He was really going to town, wasn't he?"

"He was out of control," Laura snapped.

Lucy blinked in surprise. "Ames and his brothers are champion bronc riders. He was in complete control out there. Trust me."

Was he? Laura was far from an expert on horses, but she was pretty good at reading Ames, and her gut was telling her that something hadn't gone right for him in the ring tonight.

The *Personnel Only* door flew open in the back of the building. Ames appeared, scanning the parking lot. Flint was right beside him.

Laura waved both arms at them. "Over here," she called.

The two cowboys jogged in their direction.

Ignoring Flint, Laura flew up to Ames and threw her arms around him, burying her face against his shoulder. She was overwhelmed with gratitude that he was safe.

He lifted her feet off the ground, spinning her in a full circle before setting her down again. "Thanks for coming tonight," he muttered huskily against her hair.

She couldn't believe he was pretending like everything was okay when she knew it wasn't. "Are you hurt?" She anxiously ran her hands up and down his arms.

"Nope." He hugged her close again.

"What happened out there?" She leaned back in his embrace to gaze up at him, silently begging him to tell her the truth.

He and Flint exchanged a look that was hard to read. Then he blew out a resigned breath. "One of the newbie wranglers pulled the cinch too tight on my bronc. For all intents and purposes, he gave me a real rodeo ride tonight. Fortunately, my brothers realized what was going on and helped me rein him in."

She felt the color leave her face. "I knew something was wrong the second they started doing the pickup rider stuff. You guys normally just clown around out there, but tonight felt different."

"It was." Flint raised his hat to run a hand through his hair. "And now the punk who sabotaged the strap is MIA."

Laura scanned Ames' features. "You think he did it intentionally?"

"Who knows?" Ames shrugged. "It sure looks bad for him now that he's missing."

"No kidding," Flint growled. "It'll be interesting to see if his buddy also turns up missing."

"What buddy?" Lucy glanced curiously between the two of them.

Ames gave his youngest brother a warning head shake.

Laura watched them engage in what appeared to be a silent debate. "What aren't you telling us?" She pulled away from his embrace to slap her hands down on her hips.

Ames shook his head again. "Pointing fingers won't accomplish anything. We need proof before accusing anyone of anything."

"Proof for what?" she demanded.

"Good grief!" Flint threw his hands into the air. "Just tell them already. The guy isn't worth protecting."

"Who's not worth protecting?" Laura tapped the toe of her boot impatiently.

"Your ex, that's who," Flint exploded. "The guy is a complete loser. I'm not sure why Ames is going to so much trouble to protect his name."

"Uh…maybe because your brother cares about my sister's feelings?" Lucy took a threatening step toward Flint, looking like she wanted to slap him.

Laura was more confused than ever. "What does Brex have to do with anything? I didn't even see him here tonight."

"He's pals with the punk who cinched the strap to tight on Ames' horse," Flint growled. "His only friend in town, as it turns out."

"What friend?" Laura still had no idea who they were talking about.

"Some guy named Oak. He blew into town a few months ago, whining about needing a job. Angel was kind enough to give him one, and he's been working as a wrangler for the indoor rodeo ever since."

"Oak?" Laura sought out Lucy's gaze. They knew a guy named Oak. And if Brex knew him, too, it had to be the same Oak.

"Yeah, like the tree." Flint's tone was derisive. "Apparently, it's short for Oakley."

Laura nervously bit her lower lip. "Is he kind of scrawny,

with stringy brown hair and patched jeans?" Like Brex, he'd proudly adopted the look of a gypsy.

"Sounds about right." Flint eyed her speculatively. "Why?"

"Because we know him." Laura wasn't sure what Oak was doing in Pinetop or why he was hobnobbing with Brex. "He traveled in the same caravan we did. His parents sell homemade soap and candles in craft fairs across the country." They'd never made much money at it. Oak's mom did most of the work, while his dad scared off most of their customers with his short temper and loud mouth.

Ames' blue gaze narrowed in thought. "So what's he doing in Pinetop?"

"And where is he now?" Flint's hands fisted like he was ready for a fight.

They were valid questions. Unfortunately, no one had any answers.

CHAPTER 8: FIREWORKS

4th of July

As July rolled around, the shop owners on Main Street gave their window displays a full makeover. Their red, green, and white light strands were replaced with red, white, and blue ones. Christmas trees remained up, but they were redecorated with U.S. flags, liberty bells, stars, and Uncle Sam hats.

One of the trees at the North Pole Candy Depot had been set up as a tribute to all the citizens in Pinetop who'd served in the Armed Forces. Their photos had been glued to red ball ornaments. Tiny flags were fluttering from the branches, looking like striped blossoms. The *pièce de résistance*, however, was the collection of hand-dipped chocolate pretzel stars. They were roughly the size of Laura's palm, wrapped in clear cellophane packaging, and available for purchase.

"I'll take that one." She pointed at one of the stars in the center of the tree. The prongs had been dipped in edible blue glitter.

"Would you like it in a gift box?" The grandmotherly

JO GRAFFORD

cashier lifted the chocolate ornament from the tree and laid it on a square of red metallic bubble wrap.

"Yes, please. It's for my boy...um, friend." Warmth infused Laura's face at the realization that she'd almost called Ames Carson her boyfriend. Not that he would've minded. He was certainly gunning for the position.

"I'll have it wrapped up for you in no time, hon." The woman made a work of art out of the packaging. She placed it in a blue and white striped box and tied it with a red velvet bow. When she was finished, she tastefully affixed the North Pole Candy Depot's logo sticker to the top. It was half hidden by the bow, serving as a tasteful advertisement for their amazing products without overpowering the loveliness of the gift itself.

"Thank you so much!" Laura paid for the star and carried it outside. She was meeting Ames for lunch, something they were in the habit of doing once or twice per week now. During the weeks he was in town, that is.

He was having to spend more and more time in Dallas now that their foreman had accepted a job overseas. He and his brothers weren't interviewing candidates to replace the man, either. She was both dreading and anticipating the day Ames would tell her they were returning to Dallas for good.

Away from Pinetop.

Away from me.

"Stop!" someone shouted, yanking her from her thoughts.

Laura whirled around in the nick of time to avoid being plowed into by a man in a navy sweatshirt with the hood pulled low over his face. Though his head was down, making it impossible to see his face, there was something eerily familiar about his height and build.

And then she knew.

"Oak?" She gasped out his name.

Right as he was speeding past her, he glanced up and gave her a dark glare.

It was him alright. He veered menacingly in her path, wordlessly threatening to mow her down.

As she jumped out of the way, the man chasing after him continued to shout warnings. "Stop him! He took my wallet!"

Laura's head spun in dismay back in Oak's direction, but he was gone. It was as if he'd vanished into thin air.

"He ran between the buildings!" A woman pushing a stroller pointed out the spot.

A sick feeling settled in Laura's gut. *What have you done, Oak?* Why was he back in town? Despite having a surly father, he had a God-fearing mother who'd raised him to be a gentleman. Laura couldn't imagine the sweet kid she'd grown up with turning to a life of crime. Then again, he'd tampered with Ames' bronco a while back, so it was anyone's guess what he was capable of doing these days.

She debated what to do next, knowing she was probably the only person on the sidewalk who could positively identify Oak as the thief. *Alleged thief,* she corrected inside her head, assuming the angry man who claimed his wallet was stolen had been telling the truth.

There was only one right way to handle this. With a sigh of capitulation, Laura dug out her cell phone and dialed Ames. Raising the phone to her ear, she listened while it rang.

"Hey, darling!" The sound of his voice never failed to make her heart race. "You ready for lunch?"

"I am, but I'm going to be running a little late." A howl of sirens sounded in the distance.

"Is everything okay?" he inquired quickly.

"I'm not sure. A man claimed his wallet had been stolen by a guy he was chasing. I saw who it was, so I need to give my statement to the police."

"You mean you recognized the thief?"

Alleged thief. "It was Oak." A wave of sadness swept over her. It was going to break her parents' hearts to hear he was in trouble. They were friends with Oak's mom.

"You're kidding! No one has seen hide or hair of him since my bronc riding fiasco."

"And now we know why," she sighed. "It looks like he's mixed up in something on the wrong side of the law." The howl of sirens grew closer, and a police cruiser with flashing lights pulled up to the curb. "I'm sorry about being late for lunch. Hopefully, this won't take too long."

"Where are you?" Ames sounded worried.

"In front of the North Pole Candy Depot. I was about to head to the Gingerbread House." It was only a couple of doors down from the candy store.

"I'm almost there myself. I'll come find you."

"Okay. I'll keep an eye out for you." She wouldn't mind having his moral support. Plus, the sheriff was a personal friend of his. Maybe that would speed things up a little.

It was still more than an hour before they were finally able to retreat to the Gingerbread House for a belated lunch date. They grabbed a table for two against the wall.

"I hope I'm not keeping you from anything important." Laura eyed Ames worriedly. Normally, they were finished eating by now and on their way back to their respective jobs.

"Being here for you is the most important item on my to-do list today." He reached across the table to touch his fingertips to hers.

"Even though you're about to leave town again, huh? For good this time." She wanted to bite her tongue as soon as the question left her mouth.

His expression sobered. "Who told you that?"

"Nobody." Her heart sank as she watched him. "But you're not exactly denying it."

He toyed with her fingers. "We just finished negotiating a whole new contract at Castellano's. It'll involve putting on a two to three-week show at least once every quarter. That means we won't be complete ghosts around here."

"So, you've definitely decided not to replace your foreman?" Her heart tightened with apprehension. She'd secretly been hoping he and his brothers would change their minds about that. They were leaving town, and soon.

"We're not," he affirmed in a quiet voice. "Dallas is our home, Laura. It was always our plan to return there and become full-time ranchers someday."

Her heart sank lower. "When are you leaving?" Though a waitress was approaching to take their orders, her appetite was long gone.

"As soon as we finish our current show. Couple of weeks." He paused to give their drink and sandwich orders to the waitress. Since they were regulars, they usually ordered the same thing. Despite her lack of appetite, Laura didn't try to stop him.

"I'm going to miss you." Her voice came out strained. "I already am."

"The feeling is mutual." He covered her hand with his. "Laura, I know this may be rushing things a little, but—"

"Hey! Fancy finding you here!" Brex's voice showered over them like icy rain, interrupting whatever Ames had been about to confide in her.

Laura swallowed her frustration as she glanced up to meet the half angry and half mocking gaze of her ex. "Hi, Brex." Though she hadn't laid eyes on him in weeks, she should've known he was working in Pinetop as a vendor this week. "I take it you're here for the Biggest Bang Craft Fair?"

"Sure am," he informed her in a falsely cheerful voice. "Ever since I started offering free shipping, my sales have been skyrocketing." He paused to give her a pointed look.

"You haven't stopped by my booth yet to see my Fourth of July display."

She wasn't sure what to say to that since she'd been avoiding him. He had to know that. "I've been pretty busy at the shop." She gave a vague wave of her hand.

"I can tell." He glanced between her and Ames. "Saw you talking to the police outside. Is everything okay?"

She nodded slowly, not liking the fact that he'd seen her. "Some guy claims his wallet was stolen. I was out there when he started yelling about it."

Brex's expression hardened. "Did you see who did it?"

She didn't like the look in his eyes. Instead of answering the question, she sniffed. "I have no way of knowing if the guy's wallet was even stolen. That's just what he's claiming."

When Brex didn't respond, she added, "I'm glad to hear your profits are up." She knew he needed the money for his grandparents' nursing home bills.

He gave her and Ames' joined hands a chilly glance. "Did you see the flowers I had delivered to the toy store this morning?"

"I did." She avoided meeting Ames' gaze. "It was really sweet of you to remember my mom's birthday." She wasn't sure why he'd bothered. It wasn't like he ever spoke to her parents anymore.

"I know wildflowers are her favorite. And yours," he added silkily. "Figured it might remind her of the old days." His expression grew shuttered. "Back when we were one big family, traveling from coast to coast together."

"Yeah, those were the days." *Days I don't miss one bit.* She had trouble injecting much enthusiasm into her voice. It was starting to feel like the whole point of Brex's visit to their table was to needle Ames.

Though Ames had yet to contribute a single word to the

conversation, his fingers had tightened on hers the moment Brex had approached their table.

Her ex-fiancé turned his attention to Ames. "I hear you're headed back to Dallas tonight."

Laura caught her lower lip between her teeth. That was news to her. She was both surprised and disheartened that he hadn't told her yet. Then again, maybe that was what he'd been working up to when Brex had interrupted them.

"Yep." Ames' voice was clipped.

"Whelp. Safe travels." Brex's smile didn't reach his eyes as he nodded his goodbye to them. "Maybe you'll finally find time to drop by my booth, Laura." It was a clear dig at how much time she'd been spending with Ames lately.

Laura shook her head at his retreating shoulders. "That was awkward."

"Nothing new there." Ames drummed his fingers on the back of her hand. "He's the King of Odd."

Which still didn't explain how Brex had known Ames was heading out of town again tonight, and she didn't.

She stared dully down at the table. "When were you going to tell me that you're leaving again so soon?" He'd just gotten back from his last trip.

"Over lunch today. Right before Mr. Odd showed up, actually." His voice grew resigned.

"You've never returned and left again so quickly." She blinked a few times to hold back the moisture brimming in her eyes.

"I know. I'm only here for tonight's parade. Then I've gotta get back to some ranch business I'm right smack in the middle of. So, uh..." He lifted her hand to cradle it between his. "Any chance you'd be willing to go with me?"

She whipped her head up to meet his gaze. "Come with you?" She repeated his words wonderingly.

"Yes. I know it's short notice, darling, but I'd really like to give you the grand tour of our ranch. Noelle said you can stay in the loft apartment she was using before she and Nash tied the knot."

Laura's mind raced over the possibilities. She had some more design work to do, but it could be completed anywhere she had internet access. She'd need Lucy to cover her Saturday shift, too, but she doubted her sister would mind.

"Oh, wow, Ames!" She stared at him, dazed. "I'd love to. I just need to make a few arrangements with my family." Did it mean they were taking things to the next level in their relationship even though they hadn't kissed yet?

His shoulders relaxed. "This is great!" He squeezed her hand in excitement. "Flint told me you'd say no. I can't wait to tell him he's wrong."

"I bet." They shared a chuckle over that. "From the way you and your brothers talk about the ranch, it sounds so beautiful." She smiled shyly at him. "The horses, the canyons..." *And you.* She'd be getting to see him in his element. The city he grew up in. The ranch he called home.

"Yeah, it's a pretty incredible place." He beamed at her. "You're gonna love meeting our staff. They're pretty incredible, too."

"So...tonight!" She'd have to leave work early to pack. "How long will we be gone?"

"Just through the weekend. I was planning on leaving right after the Crackle and Pop Parade. I can have you back anytime you want on Sunday." The parade was scheduled to begin at eight. It was going to be an explosive evening of lights and fun for everyone who'd arrived in town to celebrate Independence Day in Pinetop style.

And now our celebrating will continue in Dallas.

❈

"So, is it official?" Lucy excitedly dragged one of Laura's two suitcases to the Jeep and tossed it in the backseat. "Are you two finally dating?"

Laura shook her head, not wanting to attempt to qualify what her relationship with Ames was at the moment. They were more than friends. That's all she really knew.

Lucy slammed the back passenger door shut and hopped into the driver's seat. "It really stinks that the Carsons are moving back to Texas, right when things are starting to heat up between you guys."

I know, right? Laura bit her lower lip to hide her dismay. "They're not going to be ghosts, though. Ames said they just signed another contract with Castellano's. It'll bring them back for a two-week show at least once every quarter."

"It won't be the same, though." Lucy's voice was unaccountably bitter.

"Hey, look at the bright side of things." Laura attempted to inject a note of lightness into their conversation. "Flint will finally be out of your hair."

Lucy backed the Jeep from their garage, gripping the steering wheel with both hands. At the bottom of the driveway, she turned onto the main road leading into town. "And he'll flit right on to the next cute female who catches his eye. Easy come, easy go."

Laura studied her sister from beneath her lashes, surprised by her bitter tone. She was forever brushing Flint away like he was a pesky fly. "You're gonna miss him, aren't you?"

"Like a dog misses fleas," Lucy grumbled.

The Crackle and Pop Parade was already forming on the crossroads at the top of Main Street. Lucy parked behind a small plaza strip that neither of them had visited before that housed a set of law offices. Behind the building, Ames had already parked his two-toned silver pickup. He'd somehow finagled a second parking pass for them.

He stood behind his truck, waiting for them. Flint dashed into their parking spot and pretended to wave them into it like a runway attendant.

Lucy looked like she was fighting a smile as she slowly backed the Jeep in his direction. "I should run him over," she joked.

Ames jogged up to the passenger door and pulled it open for Laura. His whole face was lit up with excitement and anticipation. "How many suitcases you got with you?"

"Two, though I could've easily gotten away with one." She shot an exasperated look at her sister. "Blame it on Lucy. She made sure I overpacked."

"You're welcome." Lucy didn't bother looking their way. She was too busy glowering at Flint, who'd elbowed her out of the way to grab the suitcase she'd been about to lift from the Jeep. "Thanks to me, you're prepared for all contingencies."

Ames drew Laura into his arms while Lucy bickered with his youngest brother over the suitcases. "I'm so glad you're coming with me," he muttered in her ear, hugging her tightly.

"Me, too." For the briefest of moments, it didn't feel like he was preparing to move hundreds of miles away from Pinetop. "I promise I'll change out of my costume before we take off." Because of the Christmas in July theme of their float, she and Lucy were back in their elf dresses and stockings.

"Doesn't matter to me one way or the other," he assured her huskily. "In case I haven't told you yet today, you're my favorite elf."

She drenched him with a smile, wondering how he always seemed to know what to say to her.

The four of them walked in a cluster to the floats at the front of the parade. The staff and crew at Castellano's were manning the first three. The mayor of Pinetop was standing next to Angel Castellano in the first one. Ames and his brothers were expected to ride on the second one. They would be taking turns horsing around on a mechanical bull mounted to the center of their float.

Laura and Lucy were running the Christmas in July toy making station on the third float. The Pinetop High School student council was in charge of tossing small toys into the crowd to share "samples" of what Santa's elves were hard at work preparing for next Christmas. Nearly a dozen shop owners on Main Street had donated the miniature plush animals, squeeze balls, and other small items filling their enormous red toy sack.

The parade commenced with a spectacular performance from the Pinetop High School drum line. Darkness continued to fall as they played, enhancing the stunning display of lights on the floats following behind them.

Laura and Lucy's float was ablaze with festive strands that outlined every detail of their toy making station. In the next float, Bear Mountain Ranch had dancing bears with shimmering fur on their costumes. The North Pole Candy Depot was rolling behind them with a life-sized gingerbread house. It had animated icing on the eves, sparkling candy discs mounted to the outside walls, and a fire glowing in the hearth inside the windows. Their prancing employees tossed candy right and left into the crowd. Both local and visiting children shrieked in delight as they gathered up all the toys and goodies flying their way.

In took between twenty and thirty minutes for the parade to move at a snail's pace down the full length of Main Street. As soon as the last float cleared the finish line, the mountainside behind the shops exploded with fireworks.

A sharp whistle drew Laura's attention away from the fireworks. She discovered Ames hovering in the shadows beside the float she and Lucy were standing on.

He held out his arms to her and angled his head, indicating he was ready to depart.

Laura quickly caught her sister's eye.

Lucy mouthed a single word to her. "Go!"

Ames lifted her down and tucked her inside a waiting golf cart. Slinging an arm around her, he bent his head closer to be heard above the crack of fireworks. "I want to show you something, but we have to move quick!"

He drove through a back alley behind the shops and quickly arrived at the plaza strip where they'd started their evening. He left the golf cart parked beside the Jeep. "Flint will return it to its owners."

As soon as they were buckled into his truck, he set their course for the airplane hangar.

"You're in an awfully big hurry." Laura alternated between studying his profile and twisting around to continue watching the fireworks.

"You'll see why in a minute."

They arrived at the hangar in a little over a minute. His airplane was already idling on the runway. An attendant jogged their way to help load their suitcases.

"Already got clearance from air traffic control, sir. Your trip is a go."

Ames thanked him and tipped him. Then he bustled Laura up the stairs into the cabin.

While he folded the stairs in place and locked the door, she gazed around the interior of the luxury jet. It was faintly aglow with recessed lighting. Creamy leather seats faced each other, two on each side of the main cabin.

Ames reached for her elbow to reclaim her attention. "We'll explore the plane later." He nudged her into the cockpit, hanging his Stetson on a wall hook behind them. "You get to ride shotgun for this next part."

She gave a nervous chuckle as they strapped themselves

in. In the past, she'd been prone to motion sickness. Hopefully, this front-of-the-plane view wouldn't spark a new episode of it.

As he fiddled with the controls, she murmured, "Just for the record, I have zero flight hours as a co-pilot."

"We're about to change that, darling." Before she could blink, he had them rolling down the runway, faster and faster. They whooshed into the mountain breeze and started to ascend.

Laura caught her breath as he banked right and circled back around the side of the mountain. "Oh, Ames," she breathed, finally understanding what he'd wanted to show her.

The fireworks were still exploding, and they had the best seats in the house. As he flew them over Main Street, the grand finale flashed, shimmered, and smoked across the sky.

Without thinking, Laura reached for Ames' hand, but he was still busy at the controls. She quickly returned her hand to her lap, hoping he hadn't noticed.

"Thank you," she said softly. "That was amazing. You're amazing."

"I'm glad you liked it, darling." He sounded pleased as they continued to climb toward the clouds.

"I didn't just like it," she gushed. "I loved it. That was seriously one of the nicest things anyone has ever done for me!"

"There's that word again," he teased.

It was several minutes before they reached cruising altitude. He adjusted a few more controls, then sat back with an expulsion of satisfaction. "If the weather holds, we'll be in Dallas in a little under two hours."

The sky around them was drenched with stars. It didn't look like the weather was going to be a problem.

He leaned her way and winked. "So long as we don't hit

any turbulence, you're free to move about the cabin, Miss Lee."

"Oh!" She reached for her seatbelt. "Wow! Are you ready to give me the tour?"

"I thought you'd never ask." He held out a hand to pull her to her feet. Then he ushered her in front of him through the narrow door leading to the main cabin.

As she edged past him, it was impossible to miss the way his gaze dropped longingly to her lips.

Something inside her snapped. She was done grieving and being angry. She was done waiting for answers that might never come. She was even more done with keeping her dating life on hold because of a certain gypsy who, quite simply, wasn't worth even half of the energy she'd spent grieving over their breakup.

And, in that moment, she could no longer imagine letting Ames Carson move all the way back to Dallas without knowing what their first kiss would be like.

"Ames," she whispered, sliding her hands up his arms to clasp them around his neck.

He didn't move. Didn't immediately enclose her in his embrace. All he did was watch her. "What are you doing, darling?"

"This." Without any more preliminaries, she rose to her tiptoes to seam their mouths together.

His warm, hard lips remained still for a split second. Then they moved against hers — sampling, exploring, and taking everything she was offering him.

He kissed her like he'd waited a thousand years for it. Like he would treasure the moment forever. Like he was never going to stop.

She lost track of time while she reveled in the wonder of finally becoming his. All his.

"I can't believe you did that." He spoke huskily against her lips. "Not that I'm complaining, because I'm not."

She smiled dreamily. "Maybe I was tired of waiting."

He rocked her closer. "That makes two of us."

She wrinkled her nose at him. "You sure made me wait long enough." He hadn't rushed things between them, not even a little. And in doing so, he'd paved a clear path for her to find her way to him.

He lightly bumped noses with her. "Just wanted to make sure you were ready." He nuzzled the edge of her mouth hungrily.

"I stole our first kiss," she whispered. "The next one is up to you."

He gave her lower lip an experimental nip that made her sigh. Then he slanted his mouth across hers and took them deeper.

They kissed until a beeping sound from behind them made Ames abruptly lift his head. "I better see what's going on." He hurriedly stepped back inside the cockpit and took a seat at the controls. Then he jammed his headset back on and started barking through the microphone. "Mayday! Mayday! We're losing fuel!"

Losing fuel? How? Why? Laura shakily slid to her knees on the floor behind him, listening dazedly as he communicated with the nearest air traffic control tower.

"I know it doesn't make sense," he growled to the person on the other end of the line. "Yes, everything checked out before we took off."

She could hear the urgency in his voice, and it shook her deeply. They were thousands of feet in the air, and the plane they were in was in trouble. Unsure if they were going to make it safely back to the ground, she closed her eyes and started to pray.

❄

Fifteen minutes earlier

Hearing the drone of a small jet, Lucy glanced up and caught sight of the white lights of a plane flying overhead. Whoever it was had an aerial view of the fireworks below. Lucky them!

"It's Ames." A shadowy figure leaped up on the float beside her, making her jump. It was Flint.

She pretended to sock him in the gut for startling her like that, and he pretended to have the wind knocked out of him. Trying not to laugh, she demanded, "Did you know he had this planned?"

"Yep." He waggled his eyebrows at her. "It might not be all chocolate and roses if you hang with us Carsons, but I promise you there will never be a dull moment."

Her heartbeat stuttered at the question in his eyes, though she knew better than to give in to the tug of attraction that had always been between them. He would soon be gone. For good.

"Like appearing out of nowhere in the dark and scaring me half to death?"

"Yep."

"Smooth," she mocked.

"I thought so." He moved closer to sling an arm around her shoulders, tipping his head back to continue watching the fireworks. "Like I said, never a dull moment." His voice was low and rumbly against her ear.

She gave a long-suffering sigh. "Are you trying to flirt with me again, Flint Carson?"

"Why? Is it finally working?" he shot back.

"Not any more than the bazillion other times," she lied.

"Then, no. I'm just a friendly guy being friendly."

"Lying isn't your strong suit, cowboy." She pretended to glower at him. "Better keep your day job." For the life of her, she couldn't figure out why she didn't just step away from him. Maybe it was because it was dark outside and they were sort of alone on the float. Maybe it was because she knew he would be leaving town soon. There really wasn't a good explanation why she let him continue to hug her or why she eventually tipped her head against his shoulder.

He pulled her more snugly against his side. "Dang, you're sweet when you're not being nasty."

She made a sound of derision. "Don't read too much into it. You're leaving town soon, and I'm not." There. She'd finally pointed out the elephant in the room. Or on the float, in their case.

"We're not selling the chalets, if that's what you're asking." He rested a cheek against the top of her head. "We're gonna continue straddling Dallas and Pinetop for the foreseeable future."

But he would mostly be in Dallas going forward. "Out of fifty-two weeks in the year, how many do you honestly expect to spend in Pinetop? Eight? Twelve?" Once he and his brothers returned to running their ranch, she wouldn't be seeing much more of him. There was no way he could deny that.

"That sounds about right." He gave her shoulders a gentle shake. The grand finale of the fireworks display started, and he grew silent while the magnificent array of lights and sounds exploded across the sky. Only when it was finished did he continue speaking. "If you're willing to spend some of your vacation time visiting some cool friends in Dallas, we could easily add another couple of weeks to that tally."

"Really, Flint?" She wrenched herself from his embrace to give him an irritated look. "You're angling for a long-distance relationship with me?" *You?* She wasn't buying it. She'd pegged him for more of an out-of-sight-and-out-of-mind kind of guy.

He jutted his chin at her. "In all fairness, I've been angling for any kind of relationship at all with you. You're the one who's been dragging your feet."

She couldn't believe they were having this conversation. "Really, Flint? You blame me for being cautious? You don't exactly have much of a track record when it comes to following through with second, third, and fourth dates."

He shrugged like it was no big deal. "What's the point in wasting a girl's time after you figure out she's not the one?"

What was the point indeed! She tossed her head. Well, two could play that game. "I'm not some prospective horse purchase you can take for a test ride, Flint. Go bother somebody who's interested."

He snorted. "If you weren't interested, we wouldn't be arguing about it."

There was something about his persistence that was impressive. And appealing. And all the other things she didn't want to be feeling for a guy like him. "For the sake of this argument, let's say you're right," she said slowly.

"We both know that I am, babe."

Babe? She rolled her eyes at him. His cockiness knew no bounds. "Why should I even consider entering a relationship that is statistically doomed to fail? Long-distance romance works better in the movies than in real life." She should know. She'd been there, done that, and gotten that t-shirt.

His blond eyebrows flew upward. "I don't know what stat you're quoting, because research shows that a whopping 60% of long-distance relationships succeed."

She stared at him in astonishment. "You actually researched it?"

He faced her obstinately. "I'm trying really hard not to be insulted by that question."

As they glared at each other in the moonlight, she could see the genuine hurt in his eyes. Her lips parted to apologize.

"Sounds like you two are arguing again," a man drawled from the pavement beside the float. "Shocker."

Lucy stiffened as she recognized his voice. "If you're looking for my sister, she isn't here, Brex." Unlike Laura, she saw zero point in being nice to a jerk like him.

"Where is she?" he demanded, peering inside the float to verify her statement.

Though Lucy didn't consider her sister's whereabouts to be any of his business, she decided to tell him the truth, just so she could watch him squirm in misery. "She's on her way to Dallas for the weekend with her favorite cowboy." She wished she had some popcorn to shovel down while enjoying his reaction.

To her amazement, he dropped like a rock to his knees and started choking. Or sobbing. Or throwing up. Or some combination of those things. It was hard to tell in the darkness.

Lucy leaned over the side of the float, trying to decide if she should call for help.

Just as suddenly as he'd fallen, however, he shot back to his feet and took off running.

"Brex?" she called after him.

He didn't turn around.

Flint moved to her side to stare after him. "That was weird."

"Very weird," she agreed, chewing on her lower lip. She'd been expecting Brex's rage and maybe a bit of arrogance, not a complete emotional meltdown.

Only because she was standing so close to Flint did she hear his cell phone buzz with an incoming message.

He pulled it from his back pocket and scanned the screen.

Whatever he read made his features grow abnormally pale in the moonlight.

She reached over to touch his arm. "Bad news?"

"It's the airplane." His voice was hoarse. "Ames and Laura are in trouble!"

Lucy felt her insides grow numb as he explained that they were losing fuel. Ames had only a couple of minutes to get himself and Laura back on the ground before it was too late.

She reached for the railing on the side of the float, gripping it with both hands. There was only one thing she could do to help his brother and her sister during the short time they had left. She started to pray.

CHAPTER 9: AFTERSHOCKS

Ames listened to the set of coordinates coming through the ears of his headset. "Copy that. I'm heading that way now." A strange calm had settled over him during the past minute or two — enough to shoot off a hasty message to his brothers.

Plane is in trouble. Losing fuel. Please pray. Love, Ames

He'd added the *love* part in case he never got to see them again. Probably scared the bejeebers out of them, but there was no time to worry about that. Hopefully, they'd pray that much harder after reading it.

He could hear Laura praying on the floor behind him. Not weeping. Not acting hysterical. Just praying. He was surprised she wasn't having another one of her panic attacks.

"All of our hope is in You, Lord." Her soft, pleading voice surrounded him in the narrow space, buoying him from the darkness of his thoughts. "Whether it's our time to go, or if You still have more plans for us, I'm grateful for every moment You've given me with my parents, my sister, and Ames."

Hearing the woman he loved thanking God for him in what might be the last few minutes of her life was the most profound thing Ames had ever experienced. He gritted his teeth with renewed determination to give his attempt at an emergency landing his finest efforts. He didn't intend to give up before the last drop of fuel seeped out of their fuel tank, or the engine failed.

"Get your seatbelt on, darling," he shouted as the detour runway lights came into view. "We may be in for a bumpy landing!" The wind was picking up, rattling the jet like a rag doll. Unfortunately, they were flying straight into it.

As she scrambled to buckle into her seat in the cockpit, he caught sight of flashing, rotating emergency lights below them. First responder vehicles were converging on the runway as he got the jet into position and started to descend.

"Coming in hot," he muttered. Though he wasn't a military pilot in a fighter jet, he was heavily armed with faith, hope, and love.

And the greatest of these is love.

He replayed that short passage of scripture over and over in his head as he lowered the landing gear and performed a rapid descent. Knowing his fuel supply would shut off at any moment, he had to make each remaining second count.

Approximately twenty feet above the runway, he closed the throttles and tilted the nose of the jet upward. He touched down the main landing gear first with a light bump. The nose gear touched down next. Though a wave of exhilaration shot through him over being back on the ground, he knew it was too soon to celebrate. He applied the brakes, and the engine coughed.

And died.

"Brace yourself, Laura!" He reached for her hand, since there was nothing else he could do.

The runway turned into a taxiway as the jet flew blindly into the wind. The wind slapped head on into the nose of the aircraft, acting like a giant hand swooping from the sky to slow their speed. They reached the end of the runway and skidded past the warning lights. Once they rolled into the grass on the other side, they quickly came to a stop. The tree line was still a good fifty yards or so out. Ames knew with certainty that if it weren't for the buffeting wind, they would've kept going until they crashed.

He sat there for a moment in reverent silence, gripping Laura's hand. It was a miracle they were alive.

"Thank You, Lord." Laura whispered the words.

They went straight to his heart. He lifted their joined hands to his lips. "Yes. Thank You."

The emergency crew surrounded them the moment they stepped from the plane.

"Nice landing!" He lost track of the number of times he was high-fived and slapped on the back.

Laura gave a breathy chuckle at his elbow.

"What?" Not caring who witnessed it, he kept an arm wrapped tightly around her shoulders, unsure if he was ever going to let her go again. They were alive. It was still sinking in.

"They keep using your favorite word on you." She snickered. "I know how much you love the word *nice*."

He turned his head to press a kiss against her cheek. "Guess you've used it on me so many times that it's growing on me."

They were led to an ambulance, examined for injuries, and pronounced in perfect condition considering what they'd been through. Ames took the opportunity to text an update to his brothers.

We made it. Thanks for praying. I'll call when I can.

A pair of police detectives strode their way wearing grim expressions. "We'd like to ask you a few questions." One of the policemen remained standing by the back door of the ambulance to speak with Laura, while the other policeman walked with Ames out of earshot.

It dawned on him that something must be wrong, since the lawmen were clearly attempting to keep him from corroborating his story with Laura's story. "What's going on, officer?"

"That's what we're trying to figure out, Mr. Carson. Have you ever experienced the desire to harm yourself?"

"No." He gave the guy an incredulous look. If he was suicidal, he'd have just kept flying his plane until it crashed.

"What about the woman you were traveling with tonight? To the best of your knowledge, is she prone to bouts of anxiety, depression, or thoughts of self harm?"

"No. She went through a rough breakup about a year ago, but I wouldn't describe her as depressed. Just sad and angry, but she's getting through it."

The officer nodded and typed something into his electronic notepad. "Can you think of any reason anyone else might be trying to harm you or Miss Lee?"

Ames' breath huffed out of him. "What's this about, officer? Did you find something wrong with my jet?"

"Your fuel tank may have been tampered with, sir. Do you have any idea who would do such a thing?"

Ames reached up to run a hand through his hair. "Honestly? No."

"You mentioned Miss Lee went through a breakup. Is there any bad blood between you and her ex?"

Ames gave a dry chuckle. "I doubt I'm his favorite person, but I barely know him."

"So you haven't argued with him?" the detective pressed.

Ames shrugged. "We've traded a few mild insults. Nothing major."

"We'd like to determine that for ourselves. Would you mind giving me his name?"

"Brex Morrison."

The detective recorded the name on his notepad. "Spelled like T-Rex, but with a B?"

"Never thought of it like that, but yes."

"Is Brex short for anything else?"

"I have no idea." Ames glanced around to seek out Laura and found her still sitting in the back of the ambulance. "Laura can answer that better than me."

"Is she your girlfriend, Mr. Carson?"

"I want her to be." They'd certainly done their share of kissing before the fuel tank had started leaking like a spaghetti strainer.

"Pardon the personal line of questioning, but did Miss Lee turn down the offer to date you, sir? Even seemingly unimportant details might matter in a case like this."

"I haven't asked her yet." Ames was feeling reckless enough to do exactly that right now. "But if you want to stick around…"

The officer's lips twitched. "After the way you landed that plane back there, I'm liking your chances, sir. I'll return you to Miss Lee now."

They rejoined Laura and the second detective. He hopped down from the back of the ambulance as they approached.

"Laura, darling," Ames called to her, grinning like an idiot. "The detective wants to know if you're gonna turn down the opportunity to become my girlfriend."

She blushed. "Are you sure you're ready to be more than friends?"

"I am." He took a running leap and hopped into the back of the ambulance to slide onto the bench beside her. Though he knew she was teasing, he was anxious to hear her answer. "So, will you?"

"Will I what?" Though her eyes misted with happy tears, she clearly wasn't going to make this easy on him.

"Will you be my girl?" He gazed at her with his heart in his eyes.

"You know I will." She launched herself into his arms.

As he drew her close, he shot a triumphant look at the officers. "I reckon that's one question you can cross off your list."

The two men chuckled through the remaining part of taking their statements and quickly ended the interview.

Laura gazed around them curiously. "I know this may be a dumb question, but where are we?"

"Tucson," he supplied. "A little over a hundred miles from Pinetop."

"Oh, wow!" She flicked a glance at her cell phone. "And it's not even midnight yet."

Which begged the question of what they were going to do next. "We can either crash in a hotel for the night or have one of my brothers come pick us up. Your choice."

She pursed her lips thoughtfully. "Don't you want to stick around and deal with the repairs on your plane?"

"I wouldn't mind doing that, but if you'd rather get back home—"

"Not at all," she assured quickly. "The most important thing is that we're safe. We'll figure the rest of this out tomorrow, okay?"

He dipped his head closer to give her a lingering kiss. "Where have you been all my life?" She was so perfect for him.

"In too many cities and towns to count." She kissed him back. "I'm just glad my twisty turny path led me to you." Her voice grew dreamy.

"I love you, Laura." It felt like the right moment, so he hoped he wasn't blowing anything by laying the L word on her this soon.

"I love you, too, Ames."

The way her dark gaze grew all soft and melty told him the timing of his confession had been exactly right. Plus, she'd said it back. It didn't get any better than that.

It was another thirty minutes or so before a shuttle van arrived to take them to the pair of hotel rooms he'd managed to reserve over the phone. He helped carry her suitcases to her room and lingered outside her doorway.

"Do you want to join me for coffee or something after you get settled in?" He was still way too wound up to sleep.

"Absolutely!" She reached over to tangle her fingers with his. "I just need to call home first." She glanced laughingly down at her elf costume. "And finally change out of this. The detective who had me cornered in the ambulance asked some very interesting questions about my dress and striped stockings."

"I can only imagine." He shook his head. "If he was half as thorough in his questions as the detective who was grilling me…"

She smiled. "You got the full-blown interrogation, too?"

"Kind of felt that way." He leaned closer to touch his mouth to hers again. "I'll be back in a few minutes."

He rolled his single carryon to the room next door. The moment the door clicked shut behind him, he dialed his youngest brother.

Flint picked up on the first ring. "Is this the human version of you or the angelic version?"

"Ha. Ha."

Flint put him on speakerphone, and Nash's voice boomed across the line. "There's no such thing as an angelic version of him. You know that." His voice cracked with emotion as he added, "Man! We've never been so glad to hear from you!"

"Right back atcha." Ames was feeling a little emotional himself.

"Any injuries?"

"Nope."

"What about Laura?"

"Again, nope." He was anxious to share his other good news. "It's official now. We're dating."

Flint gave a whoop of delight. "Ol' Brex is probably gonna expire when he finds out. You should've seen him tonight after you left the float. He came looking for her. Not sure why. But when Lucy informed him she was on her way to Dallas, he hit the ground and started hacking up body organs."

"He did what?" Suspicion shot through Ames as he recalled the police detective's questions from earlier.

"Had some sort of meltdown. I don't know what else to call it." Flint didn't sound too worried about it. "When Lucy tried to help him, he jumped up and ran off."

"Strange." Ames plopped down on his hotel bed. "You want to know what else is strange? A pair of police detectives in Tucson claim there's evidence of foul play. They're saying the fuel tank on the jet was tampered with. I'm hoping to find out more tomorrow."

A moment of shocked silence followed his revelation.

"Where are you now?" Nash sounded troubled.

"Laura and I checked into a hotel here in town. Why?"

"Want us to head down there tonight?"

"Nah, that's okay. Best to get a good night's sleep first." Ames hated putting his brothers on the road for no good reason. It wasn't as if the plane would be able to undergo any repairs before tomorrow.

"Dude!" Flint finally rejoined the conversation. "Someone tried to kill you! Probably Brex, from the way he was acting."

"From the way he was acting," Ames repeated slowly, "I'm thinking he might've been trying to take me out, but not her. Think about it. He'd have no reason to assume she'd be on that airplane. However, he was very much aware that I'd be flying out tonight." He'd all but forgotten that detail until just now. "Laura and I ran into him at the Gingerbread House during lunch, and he didn't act too thrilled about seeing us together. Then, out of the blue, he wished me a safe trip back to Dallas. Not sure how he even knew I was headed out of town, but there you have it."

"I'm thinking you need to repeat word for word what you just told us to the sheriff." Nash's voice was firm.

"I intend to," Ames assured. "It's possible we're reading things into this that aren't there, but I'd rather be safe than sorry."

He and Laura had almost died tonight. Whoever was behind the tampering had taken things to a deadly level. They needed to be apprehended and brought to justice before they tried to do any more harm.

❄

Sheriff Dean Skelton strolled through the craft fair at the Pinetop Civic Center the next morning, waving at everyone who called out a howdy. He dutifully paused to sample the many jams, cookies, and crackers loaded with dip that they thrust beneath his nose. Though he was on the clock, he was enjoying himself. Patrolling the festive streets and buildings of his hometown was the fun part of his job.

Questioning a suspected felon was not. However, he owed it to the kind citizens who'd voted him into office to do everything he could to eliminate the growing crime rate in their town. It was a real shame about that jewelry heist and the series of petty thefts that had followed. It was like having a virus growing in their midst. Nothing like this had ever plagued Pinetop before. Some of the shop owners were blaming it on the all-time high number of visitors and tourists.

He wasn't convinced that was the case. If all they were dealing with was a little shoplifting, then sure. He might've agreed. But vandalizing an airplane was more than a crime of opportunity. It was personal and vindictive. It additionally had all the earmarks of being premeditated. He wasn't going to rest until he found out who'd done it.

He rounded the corner of the first line of craft booths with a full stomach, relieved to be leaving behind most of the food vendors. Strolling up the next row brought his target into sight. Though he didn't have any grounds for bringing Brex Morrison into the station for questioning, there was no law against approaching the gypsy craftsman in a public place and striking up a conversation.

Brex was engaged in what appeared to be a heated argument with a man Dean didn't recognize. The fellow was dressed similar to Brex — lots of beads, scarves, and layers. He was older than Brex by a good fifteen or twenty years, paunchier around the middle, and several decibels louder.

Despite Brex's hand waving attempts to coax the guy's volume to a more moderate level, he continued to bluster.

"I got every right to sell my candles and soaps at your booth. You owe me, and you know it!" The burly fellow proceeded to sweep an arm across the edge of Brex's table, sending one of his snowman nutcrackers flying. The tall snowman bounced to the floor with a cracking sound. His hat rolled off, and one of his twiggy arms snapped in two.

"Gentlemen!" Sheriff Skelton hurried forward to intervene. "What's going on?" Though he wasn't the least bit happy about someone creating a scene in the middle of the craft fair, the incident was providing the perfect excuse to get closer to his target.

The burly stranger whirled in his direction. "This is a private matter," he growled. As his gaze fell on the sheriff's badge, however, he seemed to deflate. "Sorry for the noise, sir." He held up his hands in surrender. "We'll try to keep it down."

"I don't believe we've met before." The sheriff placed his hands on his hips, facing the guy squarely. "Normally this many days into a craft fair, you don't see any new faces on the vendor side of things."

The large fellow ducked his head. "I was supposed to be here a few days ago, but I got delayed."

As far as Dean was concerned, that was a poor excuse for coming into the Civic Center and creating such a ruckus. No way was he letting the guy off the hook that easily. "I'm Sheriff Dean Skelton, and you are?" He held out a hand.

"Trent." The man hesitated before grudgingly shaking the sheriff's hand. He quickly let it go.

"You got a last name, Trent?" The sheriff boomed out the question in a cheerful voice. From experience, he'd learned to keep folks off guard in order to extract the maximum amount of information. He also didn't mind creating a bit of a scene, so there'd be plenty of witnesses to their conversation.

"Yeah, er, it's Burgess." Trent spared him a sullen what's-it-to-you look.

"Burgess," the sheriff repeated. "Now why does that sound so familiar? Oh, right!" He slapped his thigh so loudly that he made the guy jump. "We had a wrangler by the name of Oak Burgess working down at Castellano's for a while." Unfortunately, he'd quit his job without notice the same night he'd cinched Ames Carson's bronco too tight. "You any relation to him?" He continued to speak loudly, drawing every bit as much attention to Brex's booth as Trent Burgess had earlier. It was satisfying giving him a taste of his own medicine.

The man nodded sheepishly. "He's my kid. A bit of a klutz like his old man, but he has a good heart."

Dean wasn't ready to swallow the klutz explanation. Not

for a second. The broken snowman on the floor was no casualty of a simple case of klutziness. He knew what he'd seen.

He eyed Brex Morrison as he squatted down to gather the pieces of the damaged nutcracker. "How about you just give me a quick look at your Pinetop vendor license, sir? Then I'll be on my way."

He could tell by the man's startled blink that he'd caught him off guard again. "Well, now, officer," Trent Burgess cajoled. "What Brex Morrison and I have between us is more of a gentleman's handshake."

Meaning he didn't have a legitimate reason for displaying his products in Pinetop. "Mr. Burgess, as one professional to another, I'm sure you can understand why we require more than a handshake to participate in our craft fair." He infused a hearty mix of kindness and firmness into his voice. "If you'll just follow me to the registration table, I'm sure we can make your vendor status more official in two snaps." *After you show your proper ID and after you pay your fee, of course*. "Our event coordinators will be happy to get you set up with your own table and everything."

Trent Burgess turned a dull red. His jaw tightened, and a vein ticked in his neck. He probably knew it was no mistake that Dean's hand was resting on the handgun tucked in his holster.

"That won't be necessary, sir." He spat out his words like bullets. Yanking a knobby satchel off the floor and tossing it over his shoulder, he stepped away from Brex's booth and stomped angrily up the aisle.

Normally, Dean would've gone after him to make sure he left the building. However, Trent Burgess had made a big enough scene that there were probably enough eyes on him to ensure that happened.

Dean hung back, instead, to address the fellow he'd actually come looking for. "You alright there, Mr. ah...?" He leaned over Brex's table, pretending to get a closer look at his name tag. "Morrison."

Brex gave him a weak nod, not quite meeting his eye.

"Though we haven't formally met, I'm sure you heard me introduce myself to Mr. Burgess. So I'll get right to the point. Would you like to press charges against him?"

Brex blinked in surprise. No small amount of horror bloomed in his expression. "No way! You heard him. It was an accident."

Dean studied the gypsy craftsman thoughtfully, more than a little surprised by his response. It was as if he was afraid of the other guy. Or at least intimidated.

He tried a different tactic. "Sorry about the damage to your products." He angled his head at the broken nutcracker.

Brex gave a strained chuckle. "It happens more often than you'd think. You know…with all the kids running around and such."

"I'm sorry to hear it, Mr. Morrison, especially after the rough evening you had yesterday."

Brex's swarthy features paled. "I'm not sure what you're talking about, sir."

"Of course you aren't." Dean slapped a hand against his forehead. "Here I am yammering on and on without explaining myself." He pinned him with a bland look. "Here's what's going on. Someone reported a guy meeting your description to the medical team last night. I'm here to apologize that our paramedics failed to make it to you before you left the event. I'm also here to ensure that you're alright."

A wave of heat chased away the pallor of Brex's features. "Oh, yeah. Perfectly alright."

"Are you sure?" Dean frowned. "I heard you fell to the ground and experienced something like a seizure."

Brex stared at him for a few seconds before giving another affected laugh. "I'm kind of embarrassed to admit this, but I'd just found out that the woman I care for is dating someone else." He waved a hand dismissively. "We used to date. I was hoping to reconcile. Guess that ship has sailed." Two angry red spots appeared on his cheeks.

Used to date? Well, that was one way of describing a broken engagement. "Sorry to hear it, Mr. Morrison." That might be stretching the truth a little, but Dean was doing everything he could to increase his chances of extracting information. He started to turn away, purposely making it look like he was preparing to leave. Then he abruptly spun back in Brex's direction. "Any chance you have a pilot's license?"

Brex gaped at him. "Come again, sir?"

"A pilot's license. Do you have one?"

"No." Brex shifted nervously from one foot to the next. "Why?"

The sheriff took his time responding, rocking back on his heels to let the guy stew in his juice for a bit. "I don't normally discuss an ongoing case," he drawled, "but there was an incident at the hangar last night."

Brex continued to look uncertain. "I'm not following you, sir."

Oh, I think you are, Mr. Morrison. "Someone roughly meeting your description was witnessed coming out of the hangar." He didn't specify when, purposely keeping his fictitious story vague. "As it turns out, a fuel tank on one of the planes was tampered with."

The gypsy vendor's Adam's apple bobbed up and down. "That's impossible," he rasped.

"What's impossible, Mr. Morrison?"

"About anyone seeing me near the hangar. I've never been there. I'm not even sure how to get there." Though his words rang with sincerity, his body language suggested that he might know something about the tampering incident. Something he wasn't being very forthcoming about.

"Guess that clears your name." Dean cheerfully tipped the visor of his service cap at him. "It's always nice getting to cross another name off my list of suspects." He was doing nothing of the sort since his gut told him Brex Morrison was very much involved. Dean would just have to do a little more digging into the man's background to determine the link between him and Trent Burgess. And maybe to Trent's son, Oak.

Unfortunately, there were no security cameras mounted in the remote mountain hangar, so there was no documented evidence of who'd tinkered with the compromised airplane. The owners of the hangar had already assured him that was about to change.

He moseyed his way back to his patrol car and put in a call to the next person on his list.

Laura Lee answered right away. "Hello?" Her voice sounded hesitant.

"Thank you for taking my call, ma'am." Dean knew a lot of folks were uncomfortable with giving information out over the phone, so he got right to the point. "This is Sheriff Dean Skelton from Pinetop, trying to get to the bottom of what happened to the Carson brothers' plane last night. Are you rested up enough after your part in the ordeal to answer a few questions?"

"I am, sir." She sounded relieved to hear from him. "I'll do anything I can to help with the case."

"Wasn't your inclusion in the trip to Dallas a bit on the last-minute side?" He was still piecing together the whole story.

"It was, sir." Her voice grew breathless. "Ames Carson and I have been close friends for about a year. Yesterday, we started dating."

"Congratulations."

"Thank you, sir. Anyhow, his invitation to visit his ranch

in Dallas was part of that, I think."

"Part of what exactly, ma'am?"

"Getting to know him better. Seeing a Texas cowboy in his own environment, so to speak…" Her voice dwindled. "I'm not sure if you've heard yet, but the Carsons are moving back to Dallas soon."

"Oh?" No, he hadn't heard.

"Yes, which means we're about to be in a long-distance relationship." Her tone changed. "Sorry for rambling. I know that's not why you called."

"Actually, I think your relationship with Ames Carson might very much be a part of what's going on here, ma'am."

"What do you mean?" She sounded stressed.

"I had a chat with Mr. Brex Morrison this morning. He suffered some sort of breakdown last night after hearing you were flying with Mr. Carson to Dallas. He reportedly fell to the ground and experienced something like a seizure."

She gasped. "That sounds a little extreme. Especially since he and I broke up more than a year ago."

"Apparently, he still cares for you, Miss Lee."

"Regardless, I've given him no reason to hope we'll ever be getting back together," she protested. "It's over between us."

"The only point I'm getting at, Miss Lee, is that Mr. Morrison doesn't appear to want you dead."

A bleating sound escaped her. "That makes two of us, sheriff."

He smiled without humor. "The other point I'm getting at is that he might've been privy to the fact that the plane you were on was going to experience mechanical difficulties. Hence his extreme response to the news that you were unexpectedly on board."

She blew out a breath. "That's a lot to wrap my brain around."

"Are you acquainted with a man by the name of Mr. Trent Burgess?"

She was silent for a moment, clearly caught off guard by his rapid change of subject. "I am. We aren't close friends or anything, but my family is acquainted with him. He was part of the same group of craftsmen we traveled with for years. They think of themselves as modern day gypsies. We moved from town to town, selling our products at vendor fairs across the country."

"Until your family made a name for yourselves in the toy making industry and cut ties with the old crew, eh?"

"Oh, it was nothing like cutting ties," she assured quickly. "We're still friends with a lot of them. But I guess you could say we finally broke free."

He was more curious than ever. "Free from what, Miss Lee?"

"The cycle of poverty." She sounded sad. "Though the gypsy craftsmen are like one big family, it's a very poor family. No guaranteed income. No health insurance. No retirement. Nothing but hard work, day after day after day. Every friend you make, you leave behind. You're always a newcomer in town and a short-termer. You have no roots. It's a hard life, sheriff, one I don't miss."

"Well, it's a family that may be missing you, as demonstrated by the way they keep popping up all over Pinetop. First Brex, then Oak, and now Trent."

"I see what you're saying, sir." Laura Lee sounded uncomfortable.

"What could they possibly want from you, Miss Lee? Or from Pinetop, for that matter?"

She was silent for so long that he was worried she might be done talking.

He was wrong.

"Sheriff Skelton, I'd like to share something with you, preferably off the record."

"I'm listening." He was making no other promises. There were too many important things at stake.

"Brex Morrison is more or less coat tailing off my family's success in the toy making business. The snowman nutcrackers he's currently selling were originally my design. He stole the plans from me and started making them without my knowledge or permission. Ames Carson found out about it and wanted to report him to the vendor oversight committee to get him permanently banned from selling his products in Pinetop. I asked Ames to hold off reporting Brex, only because I happened to be aware that Brex is using the money to pay his grandparents' nursing home bills."

Intrigue rippled through the sheriff the way it always did when he knew he was close to unraveling a case. "Have you ever met Mr. Morrison's grandparents, Miss Lee?"

"No, sir."

Probably because they don't exist. He couldn't wait to start digging into the whereabouts of the grandparents. Maybe his search would finally lead to something that would connect the seemingly unrelated crimes peppering his once peaceful hometown.

"It's possible my parents met them at some point," Laura Lee offered after a pause. "I could ask them."

"How about I do it?"

"If that's what you prefer, sir."

It most definitely was. "Thank you for your time, Miss Lee. I appreciate your cooperation with the investigation."

"Of course! If there's anything else I can help with, just let me know." She sounded like a woman with nothing to hide. She certainly had plenty to lose, though, if the crime spree sweeping its way through Pinetop was allowed to continue.

They all did.

CHAPTER 10: OUT WITH THE OLD, IN WITH THE NEW

August

Laura gazed out the windows in the cockpit as the Dallas skyline drew into view. "It's never going to get old seeing everything from way up here," she breathed, gazing at the world below them. The buildings were still postcard sized. The cars in stop-and-go traffic on the highways were no bigger than ants. Interstate loops waved and twirled like roller coasters.

Ames looked pleased as he spoke to the air traffic control tower through the mouthpiece on his headset. He banked left and curled around to get the jet into position over the runway. Lowering the landing gear, he started to descend.

It was the third time Laura had flown with him to Dallas after their near disastrous first attempt, and this was fast becoming her favorite part of the trip — the swift, panoramic view of the city, followed by the inexplicable sensation of returning home. She didn't know why she felt that way about Canyon Creek Ranch after only a few visits. Maybe it was because she'd never had a place to call home until her family's move to Pinetop. Or maybe it was because Dallas was home to the man she'd fallen so deeply and desperately in love with. Or maybe it was something else entirely.

Texas was a diverse state in terms of climate and terrain. In her opinion, the Carson brothers enjoyed the best of it all by living on the outskirts of a big city. They could enjoy the sights and sounds of the metropolitan area, then leave it all behind in minutes. They owned more than a hundred very private, wooded, fenced-in acres.

She couldn't wait to be back behind their tall ranch gates. She always felt safer there.

Ames landed the plane on the runway and applied the brakes.

She experienced the pressure of being pushed back in her seat, coupled with the thrill of another successful arrival. After her first harrowing flight with him, she no longer took those things for granted.

Before long, they were rolling their suitcases to his truck parked outside the hangar. Ames gave her cutoff jean shorts and cowgirl boots an appreciative sideways glance.

"I saw that." She chuckled.

"It's your fault for being so beautiful." He unashamedly checked her out again. "Can't take my eyes off you today. Talk about distracted flying!"

"Are you angling for an apology?" She tipped her face up to him as they reached the driver's side of the truck. It was a brand spanking new Ford pickup with dual tires and an extended bed. In true Carson brother style, it also boasted a midnight blue paint job, one with a diamond sparkle finish. Definitely custom work.

He tossed their suitcases in the back. "More like a kiss." He backed her against the side of the truck and swooped in for a very tender, very thorough kiss.

"Wow," she whispered against his lips.

"Exactly what I was thinking." He kissed her again. "I'm so glad you're finally mine." He gently bumped noses with her.

She wrapped her arms around his neck. "Thanks for not giving up on me." He'd been so incredibly patient with her while she'd moped through the emotional fallout from her broken engagement. His friendship had been a very big, very important, and very precious part of her efforts to move on with her life.

"Never!" He kissed her again. "You'll always be worth fighting for, darling."

She leaned into his kiss, reveling in the way he always made her feel. "I'm so happy that it scares me sometimes, Ames."

He studied her through heavy lids. "What are you afraid of?"

"Losing you." She shivered, recalling the fuel tank that had been tampered with.

"Not gonna happen." He pulled open the door, revealing that he'd folded down the middle console into a seat cushion so they could sit closer together.

They drove with her hand curled around his arm. Since their respective jobs and his frequent travels kept them apart so much of the time, they tended to snuggle as much as they could when they were together.

The moment they passed beneath the log beam entrance of Canyon Creek Ranch, she relaxed in ways she could only do when they were together like this. "I love it here," she declared softly. "I know I'm not a native Texan, but there's just something about this place." She gazed out the windows at the pastures stretching as far as she could see on both sides of them. Cattle grazed. Horses frolicked across the grassy fields. A pair of butterflies flitted past the windshield as they rolled closer to the main farmhouse.

"Maybe it's because this is where you belong." Ames reached up to cover the hand she had resting on his arm.

She felt her cheeks turn warm as her brain immediately started to analyze what he meant by that. She couldn't help it.

Instead of parking up by the house that Nash and Noelle lived in, Ames kept driving. He circled around to the back and continued on down the paved road leading to the cabin he shared with Flint. But he didn't stop there, either. He kept on driving.

About a quarter mile further down the road, they arrived at a gravel driveway on the left that looked like it had recently been laid. A wooded lot stretched in front of them. Some of the trees had been removed from the middle to form a tidy clearing.

"What's this?" Laura gazed around them, mystified.

"It's where I want to build a house." Ames parked and opened the door. "Want to take a closer look?"

"Absolutely!" Her heart raced with excitement as he assisted her down. "I didn't know you were thinking of building. What do you have in mind?"

"Our future home." He reached for her hands. "It's all I've been able to think about lately, especially when we're apart."

"Ours?" She squeaked out the word.

"Yes. Ours." He took a knee in front of her. "I know you love me, Laura, and I know you love Texas. Will you marry me and build a life here together?"

"Oh, Ames!" She clutched his hands, feeling dizzy.

"Is that a yes?" His voice was pleading.

"Yes, it's a yes," she choked. *Oh, my goodness! This is really happening.*

"In that case..." He withdrew a small black velvet box from his pocket and popped open the lid.

A huge square diamond glinted back at her. It was mounted on a white gold band. She blinked in amazement. It looked like the same one she and Lucy had admired in the jewelry store window back in Pinetop.

"You didn't, by any chance, ask my sister for ring advice?" Her hand shook a little as she held it out for him to slide on the ring.

He grinned up at her. "She assured me this was the perfect ring."

"It is," she sighed. It was so gorgeous that her heart ached from the beauty of it. And from all the thought and effort he'd put into purchasing it. And from the enormous investment it had taken on his part. Just thinking about it made her dizzy.

"I'm just glad you like it." He stood and drew her close again.

"I love it," she declared tremulously. "But I love you even more. So much more."

As they kissed, happy tears slid down her cheeks.

He brushed them gently away. "Please assure me you're not having second thoughts."

"Not at all. I'm just a little overwhelmed right now." Her voice swelled with emotion.

"I know how close you are to your family." He tucked a strand of hair behind her ear. "They're welcome to visit anytime and stay as long as they want. If you start to miss them too much between visits, I'll fly you to the mountains for the weekend, you hear?"

"Thank you. I'd like that." So would her family. She rested her head on his shoulder, reveling in his strength and nearness.

He spun with her in his arms to face the clearing together. "Next on the agenda will be for you to help me design our dream home. I've been talking to one of the builders in town. He said we can sit down with one of his architects, and they'll sketch out anything we want."

JO GRAFFORD

"That's amazing!" She squeezed her eyelids shut, trying to absorb it all.

"You sure you're okay?" He toyed with a strand of her hair.

"If floating on clouds of happiness counts as okay, then yes."

"It counts." He reluctantly nudged her back toward the truck. "We'd better head to the house so you can say hi to Noelle. Though she never complains, I think she's been missing her friends in Pinetop. Your visit will mean a lot to her."

"Then let's not keep her waiting." Laura walked hand in hand with him to the truck. "I can't wait to share our news with her and your brothers."

"My brothers are going to give me a hard time about taking so long to pop the question." He kept up his cheerful grumbling, making her laugh all the way back to the house.

An ambulance was parked in the driveway when they arrived. Though the siren was off, its lights were flashing.

Laura's smile froze on her lips. "Noelle," she gasped, realizing it had to be close to her delivery date. "I hope she's okay."

Ames hurriedly parked on the side lawn, and they took off running toward the house. Before they could reach the porch, Noelle was rolled out on a stretcher.

"Baby's coming," she announced in a voice that was half exultant and half apprehensive. Her blonde ponytail was pulled loosely to one side.

Laura instinctively reached for her hand and started walking alongside the stretcher. "Where's Nash?"

"He's fetching my go bag." There was a catch in her voice.

"Want me to go with you guys to the hospital?" Laura wasn't sure what made her ask.

"Yes, please!" Nervous tears rolled down Noelle's cheeks.

"As difficult as my mother is, I kind of wish she lived closer right now."

"Well, you've got me as long as you need me," Laura assured. She sent an apologetic look to Ames, hoping he didn't mind.

He nodded encouragingly.

"Your future sister-in-law," Laura added shyly.

Noelle's mouth fell open. "Are you guys serious?" Despite her condition, she tried to sit up on the stretcher, eyes snapping with joy. "I'm so happy, happy, happy for you!"

"Whoa, little mama!" The paramedic held her in place.

Moments later, she was seized by a contraction that had her panting with pain. "Our little cowboy is anxious to make his appearance," she wheezed.

Nash dashed out the front door with her bag in hand. "Got it!" There was no hiding his excitement and anticipation. Nor his worry for his wife. "You hanging in there, sweetheart?"

"Yes, but hurry," she pleaded. "I don't think we have much time."

She was right.

While they were wheeling her into the E.R., Nash Dayton Carson, Junior made his noisy entrance into the world.

"My precious little Day!" Noelle reached for her baby with streaming eyes.

The paramedics gently placed her son in her arms before they finished wheeling her into the triage bay. As soon as all vitals were checked for mother and baby, they were pronounced fit to transfer upstairs to the delivery ward.

Her OB-GYN doctor rushed into the room, still gloving up. "Talk about an entrance," he complained good-naturedly. "I feel like I'm late to the party."

Flint joined them at the hospital within the hour, and they all took turns visiting with Noelle and holding the baby.

Laura had never seen three grown men so ecstatic. Nash was over the moon about being a new father, and his brothers were equally over the moon about becoming uncles. It was clear that family was very important to them.

Nash and Flint welcomed Laura to the family, as well, with crushing bear hugs.

"Got myself another sister-in-law to annoy and a new nephew to spoil rotten." Flint planted a noisy kiss on her cheek. "Best day of my life!"

Behind his joking, though, she picked up on a hint of loneliness. She imagined a guy who enjoyed being the center of attention as much as he did was starting to feel a little left out. She also couldn't help wondering where things stood between him and her sister.

Was Lucy right about him? Now that he was back in Dallas, would he simply move on like a buzzy bee to the next pretty flower? He was more complex than a lot of people gave him credit for, which made him hard to read.

Laura secretly hoped he wouldn't give up his pursuit of Lucy just yet. Maybe if he tried a little harder, he'd finally wear her down. She sure didn't mind the idea of having her sister join them in Texas. Eventually.

As soon as she had a moment alone, she dialed her sister so she could share her news.

It took several rings before Lucy picked up. "You finally remembered you had a sister, huh?"

"Giiiiirl," Laura scolded. "What kind of question is that?"

"A fair one," Lucy snapped. "You landed hours ago, and I'm just now hearing that you made it safely. Thanks a lot!"

"Oh, I'm so sorry!" Laura hadn't thought about it that way, but she should have, everything considered. "I truly am."

"You'd better be." Lucy's voice shook. "I almost lost you not too long ago."

"Well, you didn't." Laura wasn't sure where her sister's

uncharacteristic burst of worry was coming from. "You're not getting out of being my sister that easily."

Her younger sister sniffed. "So? How are things in Texas? Details, details!"

"Oh, wow! Where do I start?" Laura pushed back a handful of hair. "So much has happened already."

"I said details," her sister reminded tartly. "As in the nitty gritty—"

"Ames proposed," Laura blurted, unable to keep it to herself a second longer.

Lucy gave such a loud shriek of elation that Laura had to hold the phone away from her ear. "Well, keep talking," she commanded after she stopped shrieking. "What did you say?"

"I said yes." Another ear-splitting scream on the other end of the line made her wince. "Right afterward, Noelle went into labor, and Nash Dayton Carson, Junior arrived into our lives. They're calling him Day for short."

"That's so precious," her sister moaned. "I'm assuming he came out of the oven as good looking as all the other hunks of burning Carson?"

"Lucy," Laura spluttered, blushing.

"Hey, you know it's true. Otherwise, you wouldn't be marrying one of 'em."

"That's not the only reason." A giggle of happiness bubbled out of her.

"But it's one of them," her sister insisted.

Laura glanced around the nearly empty waiting room and shielded the mouth piece before responding. "Pretty sure Flint is feeling a little left out. He's happy for everyone. Don't get me wrong, but a little sad at the same time, if you know what I mean."

Her sister was silent for a moment. Then she sniped, "He *would* try to make it all about him."

"No, I think it's more than that." Laura wasn't sure how to

make her understand. "Maybe you could give him a call tonight and try to cheer him up."

Lucy made a huffing sound. "Pretty sure he's forgotten all about me already."

"Pretty sure you're wrong." It was just a gut feeling, but it was a strong one.

"I'll think about it." Lucy sounded noncommittal.

Disappointment flooded Laura. She heard the *no* even though her sister didn't come right out and say it. "You do that. I love you! Gotta call Mom and Dad now."

Her parents were beside themselves with happiness for her and Ames.

"Oh, Laura, honey," Ayaka Lee sighed. "He's the right one this time."

"I know." Way down deep, she knew it was true.

❄

September

Pinetop was reverberating with excitement again. Autumn was a new season, so it ushered in the next wave of festivities across the small mountain town. First, they hosted the Harvest Hop down at the Civic Center. It was followed by their annual Back to School Bash, a carnival that lasted a full weekend. Soon afterward, Bear Mountain Ranch opened its cornfield maze and pumpkin patch.

Laura's newest toy designs had been an instant hit when her family had first unveiled them last summer. She was preparing to roll out a whole new autumn version of it, complete with scarecrows and cats to clip to the fences.

The only thing that dimmed the joy of the season for her was the continued string of thefts being reported by the local shop owners. They'd plagued the town all summer and were showing every sign of continuing into fall. It was a pity that their once peaceful town was grappling with something so sinister.

Though the local news reported them as petty thefts, probably to keep the fear factor down, quite a few higher ticket items were included in that statement — jewelry, figurines, and collectible coins and stamps. Shop owners were securing more and more items inside locked, glassed-in cabinetry. Extra security cameras were installed from one end of Main Street to the other, even at the toy store where she and her family worked.

Laura hated having to be so careful about everything, but it couldn't be helped. This was the new normal in Pinetop.

The entrance bell jangled, announcing the arrival of a new customer. Laura glanced up from her easel. "Welcome to Santa's Toy Factory!" The words died on her lips when she saw who it was.

Brex Morrison moved her way with his hands stuffed in the pockets of his double-breasted blazer. "Is it true?" He searched her features as he drew closer.

"Is what true?" She glanced across the room to gauge how far away her sister was. Lucy nodded at her from the play zone to let her know she was aware of their unexpected visitor.

Brex had been absent from town ever since Laura's engagement to Ames. She'd been sort of dreading their next confrontation. And now she was simply anxious to get it over with,

"Rumor has it that Ames gave you a ring that belongs in a safe deposit box." His mouth twisted in disapproval. "Kind of hard for me to compete with that."

"It wasn't a competition." She spoke through stiff lips. "You and I weren't meant to be. That is all."

"Is that why you kept the ring I gave you?" His dark gaze glinted with anger.

She stared blankly at him. "What are you talking about?"

"Just for the record, I'm not mad that you didn't return it." He removed his hands from his pockets and spread them beseechingly. "All this time, I was hoping it meant you intended to put it back on." He huffed out a long-suffering breath. "That is, after you punished me long enough for my mistake in letting you go."

Laura's insides churned sickly. "You didn't let me go, Brex. You intentionally ended our engagement. I've never understood why, and I probably never will, but it no longer matters."

"It matters to me!" He sounded incensed.

She ignored his impassioned words. "I'd honestly forgotten about the ring. If you'd like it back, I'll try to remember where I put it." She shook her head. It seemed so long ago since she'd taken it off.

"Man!" He snorted. "It must be nice to have so many rings you can't remember where you put them."

She saw no point in responding to that.

His dark gaze fastened at last on her engagement ring. "You really should put that somewhere safe."

"It's insured." She moved her hand so he could no longer see the ring. His scrutiny of it was making her uncomfortable. She wished he'd leave the store.

"Doesn't matter," he growled. "With all the thefts happening around here lately, it's foolish to make yourself a target."

Her lips parted in astonishment. "I'm no longer your concern, Brex." He'd given up that right more than a year and a half ago.

"You'll always be my concern, Laura, like it or not!" With that cryptic comment, he spun around and left the shop.

While Laura stared after him, her sister joined her at the easel. "That was unnerving," she confessed. "I knew he wouldn't be happy about my engagement to Ames, but..." She shook her head.

"His opinion doesn't matter." Lucy's eyes snapped with anger. "Not anymore."

"I almost wish I hadn't offered to give back his ring," Laura muttered. "I was so upset the day I took it off that I have no memory of what I even did with it."

"You didn't do anything with it." Her father moved silently across the room to join her and Lucy. "You left it on the table in the RV. Your mother and I found it and put it away for safekeeping."

Laura pressed a hand to her chest in relief. "Oh, good! Where is it now?"

"With Sheriff Skelton, I'm afraid."

"Why?" Laura was confused.

"Because it was stolen."

"Stolen," she repeated, quaking.

"Yes. And the last thing your mother and I wanted was for you to be accused of having anything to do with taking it — not after working so hard to leave that mess behind us."

Laura nearly toppled off her stool. "What mess? What are you talking about?"

"It's a long story. The short version is, I promised to call the police the next time I laid eyes on Brex Morrison. They're on their way now to arrest him."

A wail of sirens sounded outside the store windows. Laura scrambled down from her stool. She hurried to the front of the store with Lucy on her heels.

Sure enough, Brex was being held spread eagle against the side of a police cruiser.

"It's over, my precious girls." Akaya Lee materialized at

Laura's side and slid an arm around her middle. She held out her other arm to Lucy, who quickly joined their huddle.

"What's over?" Laura still wasn't clear about what they were witnessing.

"Brex is a jewelry thief. So are Oak and Trent Burgess. They'll be going away for a long time. He won't be bothering you anymore."

"I can't believe it." Laura's heart skipped a few beats at the realization that she'd almost married a criminal. A man she'd kissed. A man she'd once trusted with her life.

"I can." Lucy's voice was bitter. "There's always been something about him that rubbed me the wrong way. I just didn't know what it was until now."

"Be that as it may, your father and I were taken in by him at first, too." Their mother hugged them tighter. "You weren't the only one, Laura. He talks a good game. Beneath all of his Old World charm, though, is a very dangerous man."

Laura shivered, unable to deny what she was hearing. However, her horror was accompanied by no small amount of sympathy. "I wonder what's going to happen to his grandparents now that—"

"There were no grandparents," her mother sighed. "Or any nursing home. He made up that story to keep you from reporting the theft of your toy designs to the police." Her voice turned bitter. "And the reason he stole them was so he'd have a place to hide all those stolen pieces of jewelry."

Laura drew a pained breath. "You mean inside the snowmen nutcrackers?"

"Bingo. It was so much easier to carry and mail the stolen goods around undetected that way."

There were so many layers to Brex's deception that it was difficult to keep them all straight. The one Laura still didn't understand was where she'd fit into all of it. Had he truly fallen in love with her, or had that been just another layer of deception?

"I know what you're thinking, Laura, and I wish I knew what to say to make you feel better." Her mother's voice was soft.

"Do you think any of it was real?" It certainly had been on Laura's part. "Do you think he felt anything for me at all?"

"I do." Regret echoed in her mother's voice. "If he didn't, I doubt the sheriff would've been able to link him to the tampered fuel tank on Ames' airplane."

Laura's knees grew weak at the reminder of just how far her ex had been willing to go to get her back. He'd been willing to kill for her! She drew a shuddery breath. "How many more gypsy craftsmen were involved in the thefts?" She was almost afraid to ask.

"We're not sure, hon." Regret echoed in her mother's voice. "All I can tell you is there were some bad eggs in that basket. That's the real reason we cut ties with the group and moved to Pinetop. For years, we'd suffered break-ins to our cash box. We knew it had to be an inside job, because it continued to happen no matter how many state lines we crossed. When Brex followed us here and the thefts started up again, we realized he must be part of it. The moment Sheriff Skelton approached us, we told him everything." She shuddered. "We should've gone to the law sooner. We thought we were protecting our family by keeping quiet. In the process, we almost lost you." She hugged Laura tighter.

"But God had other plans for us," Laura assured softly.

"But God," her father echoed, joining them in front of the window.

It was a long time before any of them spoke again. They watched in eloquent silence while Brex was handcuffed and driven away, each adrift in their own thoughts.

Laura's mother pressed a kiss to her temple. "Would you like me to make you a cup of hot tea or coffee?"

"Yes, please." She was desperate for something to warm her from the inside out. "I don't care which. Just surprise me."

"I'll help. I could use a shot of caffeine myself." Lucy followed their mother to the break room in the back.

Laura gave her father a grateful look. "Thank you for bringing our family to Pinetop." She could only imagine the number of friendships he'd been forced to sever in the process. For him, the move had been the end of a whole way of life.

"It was the right thing to do." His voice was flat with conviction.

"Was it hard?" She moved closer so she could lean her cheek against his arm.

"At first, but it became easier as we watched you and Lucy settle in." A faint smile curved his lips. "You deserved a better life. Pinetop is everything we wanted for you girls and more."

"What about Texas?" She playfully elbowed him.

"I'm still getting used to the idea." He shook his head woefully at her. "A little patience, please?"

"Ames wants you and Mom there for Christmas." Her voice was beseeching.

"So I've heard."

"You mean he's already asked you?" Laura leaned away from him in astonishment to get a better look at his expression.

Her father treated her to a mock glare. "Every time that boy approaches me, he's got another request." He spread his hands. "May I marry your daughter? Would you like me to build you an in-law suite in our new home? Will you visit for Christmas? Demands! Demands! Demands!"

"Oh, you have it rough, Dad!" Laura shook her head in mock sympathy. "A future son-in-law who keeps you in mind with every major decision he makes. So rough!"

"I know." Her father tucked her against his side again. "Like I said, it's going to take some getting used to."

EPILOGUE

December

It was Pinetop's most favorite time of year again. The shop owners on Main Street kicked off the winter season with yet another parade. It was followed by a Snowball Jamboree. Since the first snow of the year had yet to blanket the mountain, baskets of handmade plush snowballs were handed out to the children, and a highly energetic snowball fight ensued in Town Square.

The official tree lighting ceremony was placed on the calendar, and a flurry of preparations began for the St. Nicholas Dance Off that would follow later that evening. The dance off was a new event. Pinetop's event committee was always coming up with more ways to celebrate the holidays. All the young singles in town were really looking forward to it.

In the meantime, a very special event was taking place for two no-longer-single residents. Technically, one of them was no longer even a resident. Laura and Ames were getting married.

And today was the day.

Laura stood in the dressing room off the vestibule of the First Church of Pinetop, hardly able to believe it was finally her turn to be a bride.

After one very big false start on my way here…

As soon as the thought popped into her mind, she forced it away, not wanting to give Brex and his accomplices any undeserved head space on such a special day. They'd been transferred to a higher security prison in Phoenix, so they weren't going to be causing any more trouble for her and Ames. Regardless, she was looking forward to moving to Dallas and putting more miles between them.

Lucy glided her way to adjust her wedding veil. "Dare I ask what that little pucker on your forehead means?"

"You don't want to know." Laura shivered and willed all final thoughts about the jewelry robbers out of her mind.

"It's over. He can't hurt you anymore. None of them can."

"I know." Laura gave Lucy a reassuring nod in the mirror. She should've known her sister would be able to pick up on her fretting. They'd always possessed an uncanny ability to read each other's thoughts.

"You deserve this, so try to be happy," Lucy begged softly. "Please be happy."

"I am." It was true. Laura's gaze dipped to the antique lace gown they'd picked out together at a local resale shop. If there was any truth to the story, it had been donated by a celebrity singer while passing through town to perform at Castellano's. "I'm so happy I can hardly stand it," she confessed. That was the part that scared her the most. She hadn't realized it was possible to feel…so much.

"Tough." Lucy rolled her eyes as she adjusted one of the pleats in her bridesmaid dress. She looked amazing in the sage green column gown. They'd selected a design with a classic empire waist and a skirt that draped to the floor.

"You say the sweetest things," Laura teased. "No wonder Flint is so bewitched by you."

To her surprise, Lucy burst out laughing. "You're not wrong. We're both brats, aren't we?"

Brats who belonged together, in Laura's opinion. She hoped her sister figured it out before it was too late.

The door opened and shut, and Noelle joined them. "Sorry for the disappearing act." She tugged uncomfortably at the top of her dress. "Day was ready to nurse again, and..." She bit her lower lip. "Too much information, I know. Sorry."

"No need to apologize. Everything that's said in the bride's dressing room stays in the bride's dressing room," Lucy promised as she helped her smooth out the front of her gown. "You look beautiful, little mama."

Noelle frowned critically down at herself. "Not too fat?"

"No!" Laura and Lucy chorused the word so fiercely that Noelle's expression relaxed.

"Thank you for saying that," she sighed.

Mrs. Lee breezed into the room next, looking tearfully joyful. "My precious girls!" She held out her arms to them, and her two daughters stepped into her embrace. "You, too, Noelle. We're about to become family."

Noelle gave her a grateful smile and joined their group hug.

Ayaka Lee sent up a prayer of thanksgiving over the ceremony about to take place. Then she prayed a special blessing over the days to come.

"Amen." The four of them solemnly spoke the last word together.

Mr. Lee knocked on the door only seconds later to walk his wife down the aisle. Then Nash came to escort Noelle. Though he was serving as Ames' best man and Lucy was serving as Laura's maid of honor, he'd insisted on walking his own wife down the aisle. They would make the switcharoo and take their correct positions once they reached the altar.

Flint came to collect Lucy next.

He crooked an arm at her, silently drinking her in the way Ames was forever doing with Laura.

Lucy merely rolled her eyes at him as she laid her hand on his arm. "We seem to be making a habit of this." They'd served together at one other wedding a few months earlier.

"Practice makes perfect," he quipped, wrapping her hand more firmly around his arm.

"You wish," she hissed at him.

"More than you know," he retorted.

Laura watched a blush stain her sister's face as Flint led her away.

Then it was her turn. Her father reappeared in the doorway.

"May I have the honor?" His dark eyes were as damp with emotion as mother's had been as he held out an arm to her.

She squeezed his arm affectionately and moved with him into the vestibule. "Thank you, Dad. For everything you did to get me here. For raising me. For loving me. For giving me faith. I'm so grateful for the life you and Mom have given to Lucy and me."

"It's been our honor and pleasure to raise you both." He patted her hand. "I just wish you girls hadn't grown up quite so fast on us."

They made their way to the entrance of the sanctuary. The pianist flicked a glance their way from the platform and started playing the opening notes of the wedding march.

Haruki Lee proceeded to lead his oldest daughter down the center aisle to the altar, where her favorite cowboy was eagerly waiting for her.

Laura breathlessly met his gaze. What she saw in his eyes made her feel boneless, like she was floating the rest of the way to him on a wave of pure joy. She knew she looked her best, but it was his love that made her feel beautiful, today and always.

"She's the best part of me, son." Her father's voice cracked as he handed her over to her groom. "Treasure her always."

"I will, sir."

Laura exchanged vows with the man of her dreams and pledged herself to him for the rest of her life. He was the one. He was worth it.

Ames sealed their promises to each other with a tender brush of his lips against hers. "And to think this all started with a stolen kiss," he teased.

But it was so much more than that. They both knew it.

❋

Two weeks later

AMES AND LAURA SQUEEZED IN A HONEYMOON AT THE coast. Then he flew them back to Pinetop to participate in his and his brothers' last week of performances for the year at Castellano's. They stayed so busy cramming in last-minute lunches and dinners with her parents and other friends around town that Flint felt like he was still exercising the horses and doing most of the preparations alone.

Not that Ames didn't deserve to be happy, but still...

Flint clapped on his Stetson as he exited the dressing room, trying not to dwell on the real reason he was so irritable. Tonight's show held an extra note of finality for him, since their next performance wouldn't be until March. The idea of not seeing Lucy for that long made him feel every way but the right way.

She'd all but stopped talking to him after the wedding,

and the new level of distance she'd placed between them was killing him. He would do anything to change it, but it wasn't something he could do on his own. If Lucy truly didn't want to date him, there was only one course of action left. He was going to have to let her go.

The thought was eating away at him, stealing his peace and poisoning his existence. He didn't want to face a future without her in it. He craved her smart mouth too much. Maybe it was a dumb reason to fall for a woman, but her insults always made him feel more alive. Special. Like he mattered.

"Dude," one of the new wranglers hollered up the aisle at him. "Isn't that white trailer in the parking lot yours? 'Cause it needs to be moved ASAP. It's blocking the entrance ramp."

Flint scowled in surprise. Though it was true that the horse trailer he and his brothers owned was white, they kept it parked at the far end of the lot. Whatever trailer was blocking the ramp wasn't theirs. Just in case, though, he headed toward the exit to have a look at it.

To his consternation, the white trailer parked at the top of the ramp was indeed theirs. *What in the world?* Unable to explain how it had gotten there, Flint hurried up the ramp. Since he'd left the building coatless, he intended to get to the bottom of the mystery as quickly as possible. Surely, there was a reasonable explanation.

When he reached the top of the ramp, his first observation was that the rusty, dented pickup it was hitched to didn't belong to the Carsons. His second observation was that an identical white horse trailer was parked on the far side of the lot where it always was. His shoulders relaxed. The one parked in front of him wasn't theirs.

Feeling even more mystified than before, he stalked around the trailer, approaching the driver's door of the truck from behind.

Before he could peek through the window, the door swung open.

"Whoa!" He had to dance out of the way to avoid being hit.

Lucy Lee hopped down to the ground, looking grim. Her eyes landed on him and rounded with uncertainty. "What are you doing here?"

His eyebrows rose. "Making sure our horse trailer wasn't blocking the entrance ramp. They're pitching a fit about it inside." He waved at the trailer. "What's going on?" Why was she driving it? Did it belong to her?

"Don't ask." Her voice was flat.

"Already did."

"It's a long story."

"One I unfortunately don't have time to hear," he growled. "They're about ready to call a tow truck." Tonight's show would begin in less than two hours.

"You think I don't know that?" She glared at him as she moved around him and tried to pop open the hood. Despite multiple attempts, it didn't budge.

With a huff of impatience, he nudged her out of the way and popped the hood for her.

"I could've done that," she muttered, peering beneath it. She puttered over the battery.

He glanced away, trying not to think about how hot she looked beneath the hood of a truck. She'd made it painfully clear that his hopeless attraction to her wasn't going anywhere.

Her sigh of despair still managed to tug at his sympathies.

Swinging his head back in her direction, he barked, "Something I can do for you?" She might not want his help, but it sure looked like she needed it.

"I don't know." She bristled at his tone of voice, waving a hand vaguely at the tangle of equipment beneath the hood.

"It won't start." She drew back a leg and viciously kicked the bumper.

Flint was unable to hold back a snicker. "Want me to try to start it now?"

"Very funny!" Her glare deepened. Unless he was mistaken, there was an underlying hint of fear in it, too.

Grimacing, he leaned around her to have a look and almost immediately zeroed in on the problem. One of the battery wires was loose. He tightened it down. "Now try it."

She stomped around him to climb back inside the truck and turned the key. The engine roared to life.

He shut the hood for her and dusted his hands.

The truck and trailer jerked forward. The way she kept feathering her brakes made him wonder if she'd ever driven a hitch before. He watched her narrowly miss clipping the bumper of another vehicle as she inched her way to the far side of the parking lot. With a puzzled grunt, he followed her. No, her business wasn't any of his business, but he still couldn't bring himself to head inside until he was sure she was okay.

Which he was pretty sure she wasn't.

She parked and hopped down from the truck again, double checking the door handle to make sure it was locked.

He could tell by her agitated movements that she didn't realize he was standing there. Not wanting to startle her, he cleared his throat to make her aware of his presence.

She whirled around, blinking at him. "Flint?" For a moment, she looked so lost that he did the first thing that came to mind.

He leaped forward and took her in his arms. To his enormous surprise and gratitude, she let him. They stood there in silence, just holding on to each other.

He was the first to speak. "Any chance I can talk you into driving this rig all the way to Texas for Christmas?"

Instead of answering, she burst into tears.

Man! His heart constricted as he tightened his arms around her. He wished he knew what he'd done wrong. Why everything that came out of his mouth lately seemed to push her further away.

"There's nothing left for me in Pinetop," she quavered against his chest. "Not with Laura leaving."

He was aghast by the bleakness in her voice. "What about your parents?"

She sniffled loudly. "Ames keeps offering to build them an in-law suite in Dallas, and I think they're actually considering it."

"You're kidding!" He couldn't imagine the Lees leaving Santa's Toy Factory behind. They were the biggest reason it was such a roaring success.

"I'm not sure about anything anymore." Lucy clung to him, shivering.

His heart thumped at the realization that, regardless of what was troubling her, she felt safe with him. The smart-mouthed Lucy Lee, who was usually pushing him away, was now pulling him closer. She was the biggest puzzle he'd ever encountered, a Santa-sized list of contradictions and complications that he'd gladly spend the rest of his life figuring out.

But she'd said no, and he respected that.

He'd been hoping like crazy to cross paths with her one last time before leaving town, so he could say goodbye. The way she was plastered against him, though, was making a whole new set of possibilities swim through his head.

He reached up to trail his hand down the long, glorious, white-blonde strands of her hair. It was something he'd never dared to do before. "May I kiss you?" Emotion roughened his voice. He'd never before seen her this unraveled, this vulnerable.

She tipped her face up to his. "Why not? Heaven knows you've been wanting to for as long as—"

He silenced her by claiming her lips. Though an icy breeze was swirling down the side of the mountain, a special brand of light and warmth blazed between them, just like he'd always known it would. She was soft and pliable in his arms, tearful and giving. She was every one of his dreams come true.

Shoot! In that moment, he would've willingly ripped his heart out of his chest and handed it to her if she'd asked him to.

She pulled her mouth from his way too soon. "Goodbye, Flint." Tears choked her voice as she slid from his embrace.

Wait! What? He stared after her, dazed, as she walked toward the dinner theater alone.

"Lucy!" He jogged after her, unable to accept that it was over between them. Not after what they'd just shared. "We need to talk." He leaped in front of her, jogging backward.

She waved a gloved hand helplessly at him. "Don't you need to get downstairs to the stable?"

"Yes, but—"

"Don't worry, cowboy. You'll forget all about me after you're gone." There was a world of sadness in her voice that reached beneath his rib cage and squeezed the one organ in the world that beat just for her.

Frustration clogged his throat. "If you wanted me to forget you, you shouldn't have kissed me."

She looked stricken. "I'm so sorry—"

"I'm not," he snarled.

"Yo, Flint!" someone shouted from the bottom of the ramp. "You're needed down here pronto!"

He gnashed his teeth at the interruption and hollered back, "Be right there!" To Lucy, he pleaded, "How about we grab a cup of coffee after the show?"

"Sorry, cowboy." She blinked rapidly, looking like she was

trying not to break down. "I don't plan to hang around that long."

He was torn between his duties and the agony of leaving her like this. "Listen, if you're in any sort of trouble—"

"I'm fine," she said quickly. Too quickly. "Go be amazing out there tonight, Flint Carson."

The fact that she'd kissed him *and* she was being nice to him only served to amplify his concerns. Yeah, something was wrong alright. "Listen." Though he remained in her path, he stopped jogging backward, forcing her to halt. "I'm gonna go put out whatever fire is happening inside. Then I'll be right back to get to the bottom of whatever is troubling you, you hear?"

"My hero," she mocked, dabbing at the edges of her eyes.

He scowled at her cavalier tone. If she didn't think he was going to keep his word to her, then she knew nothing about the Carson brothers.

Sprinting back down the ramp, he yanked open the door to the stable, anxious to handle whatever needed to be handled so he could return all the sooner to her.

"Surprise!" The entryway erupted into cheers. His heart sank as the reason became apparent. The Castellano's staff was throwing a surprise goodbye party for him and his brothers. There were banners hanging on the wall, a life-sized card that everyone had signed, and the biggest table of desserts he'd ever laid eyes on.

"Wow!" Flint gazed around the hall, deeply moved by their outpouring of appreciation and friendship. "You do realize we're gonna be back for a show in March?"

Roman Rios strode his way to deliver a teeth-rattling back slap. "It won't be the same, and you know it. We're gonna miss having you here full time. It's been a real honor working beside each and every one of you Carson brothers."

His words were met with claps and cheers of agreement.

Since there was no fire to put out, after all, it wasn't easy for Flint to break away. When folks threw a party in your honor, you were kind of expected to be present. He didn't manage to slip back outside until a few minutes before the show was supposed to begin.

To his intense disappointment, Lucy's beat-up brown truck was no longer in the lot. He tried to take comfort in the fact that her white trailer was still parked beside his. He turned dejectedly back to the building, knowing now he'd have no choice but to catch her after the show.

If she's still here. Which she'd vowed she wouldn't be.

The thought of never seeing her again was unbearable. He slid to his knees on the cold pavement and did something he'd been meaning to do for a while. He wasn't sure what had taken him so long, other than his own stubbornness.

"God, it's me. Flint Carson. I know You don't hear from me often, and I'm gonna work on that. In the meantime, I'm begging You." He couldn't bear the thought of the woman he loved hightailing it out of town while he was in the ring. "Help me find a way to help Lucy." Whatever she needed, he'd give it to her if only she'd let him.

A sense of peace settled over him. He wasn't sure if it had anything to do with his simple prayer. Maybe it was just so cold outside that it was taking the edge off his worries. Numbing them or something.

However, he liked the idea of having God on his side when it came to his pursuit of Lucy. It was something he hadn't tried before, and it felt good. It felt right. Like he might finally have a shot at succeeding with her where everything else had failed.

❄

Dallas bound

THE FLIGHT HOME AFTER THE SHOW WAS A FULL ONE. NASH was present with Noelle and their snoozing son. So were Ayaka and Haruki Lee.

Laura was seated beside Ames in the cockpit as usual. "Merry almost Christmas!" She bent over his captain's chair to press a kiss to his cheek.

He turned his head to capture her lips instead. "I love you, Mrs. Carson."

His kiss packed such a wallop that her knees felt unsteady by the time she slid into the seat beside him and reached for her seatbelt. "I love you, too." She was ecstatic about the prospect of spending their first Christmas as a married couple in Texas. She had no idea how he'd talked her parents into traveling during one of the busiest times of the year at the toy store. She was simply grateful he'd pulled it off. Only one person would be missing from their holiday celebration.

"What's wrong?" Ames started his pre-flight sequence at the controls.

"Lucy," she murmured. Lately, her sister had been acting, well...off.

Ames continued to work the controls. "Don't give up on her yet. As long as Flint remains in Pinetop, there's hope he'll convince her to change her mind."

She blinked at him. "I thought he was leaving tonight, as well."

"He is." He shook his head, chuckling. "But if there's one thing I've learned about my youngest brother, it's to never underestimate him. Flint Carson is full of surprises."

"This isn't something that can be solved by one of his pranks," Laura sighed. *Nobody wishes he could more than me.*

"Oh, come on!" Ames reached for her hand. "It's almost Christmas, the season of miracles. All you have to do is believe."

"You're right." She placed her hand in his. "And I do." At least she was trying to.

"In that case, I have a prediction to make. You'll be reunited with your sister by Christmas."

Laura wished she shared his faith. Though she knew he was only trying to distract her, she smiled as he drew her fingers to his lips and kissed them one by one.

And then it hit her. Her new husband wasn't one to be underestimated, either. He probably had enough faith for both of them.

She felt herself falling in love with him all over again as they started rolling down the runway toward Christmas and home.

❄

Thank you for reading
Cowboy Stolen Kiss for Christmas.

Want to know just how far Flint will go to lasso a date with Lucy?

Find out in
Cowboy Accidentally Hitched for Christmas

SNEAK PREVIEW: COWBOY ACCIDENTALLY HITCHED FOR CHRISTMAS

Anxious to make it home for Christmas, a rodeo star hits the road in a hurry, only to discover he's hitched his truck to the wrong trailer!

In his defense, it's the same model and color as his. Plus, it's dark outside. Not to mention he's trying to beat a snowstorm out of town.

At the next truck stop, he finds himself face-to-face with the trailer's very lovely, very angry (and slightly terrified) rightful owner…and soon finds himself offering to make it up to her by posing as her husband for the remainder of the road trip. Yeah, she has her reasons for begging that kind of favor. Good reasons. And though he's always been a sucker for damsels in distress, her situation feels like more than that— a whole lot more, at least where his feelings are concerned.

❅

Pick up your copy here:
Cowboy Accidentally Hitched for Christmas

This series is available in eBook, paperback, and Kindle Unlimited on Amazon!

AUTHOR'S NOTE TO THE READER

Dear Reader,

Thank you for buckling up for another ride with the Carson brothers. If you have siblings, you can probably relate to their endless teasing and rivalry. I sure can! I'm one of five siblings, myself.

My all-time favorite sibling memory occurred after my oldest sister left for college. She visited home for Christmas, pulled out a nutcracker while playing a family game, and accidentally sent a pecan flying off the edge of the table. She crawled under the table and couldn't immediately locate it, so she hollered, "Does anyone see a nut under the table?"

The remaining six of us ducked our heads to look at her still on her knees under the table and burst out laughing. Yes, we saw the nut alright!

Because this book is gearing up for the grand finale in the next book, I wrote a super fun and angsty Bonus Epilogue to peel back a few more layers on another pretty tough nut — Flint Carson. He's a handful, I know, but he has a heart of gold beneath all the cockiness. And horsing around. And pranks. Claim your copy of the **Cowboy Stolen Kiss for Christmas Bonus Epilogue** here.

If you're having any trouble tapping on the bonus story, please type https://BookHip.com/MXQJHGF into your phone or computer browser.

Thank you for reading and loving my books!

ABOUT THE AUTHOR

Jo is an Amazon bestselling author of sweet and inspirational romance stories about faith, hope, love and cowboys with a few Texas-sized detours into humor. She also writes sweet and inspirational historical romance as Jovie Grace.

1.) Follow on Amazon!
amazon.com/author/jografford

2.) Join my Cuppa Jo Readers group!
https://www.facebook.com/groups/CuppaJoReaders

3.) Follow on Bookbub!
https://www.bookbub.com/authors/jo-grafford

4.) Follow on Instagram!
https://www.instagram.com/jografford/

5.) Follow on YouTube
https://www.youtube.com/channel/UC3R1at97Qso6BXiBIxCjQ5w

        amazon.com/authors/jo-grafford
        bookbub.com/authors/jo-grafford
        facebook.com/jografford
        instagram.com/jografford
        pinterest.com/jografford

ACKNOWLEDGMENTS

Many thanks to my sweet editor and friend, Cathleen Weaver, to my beta readers Mahasani and Pigchevy, and to all the other amazing Cuppa Jo Readers on Facebook!

JO'S TITLES

A Very County Christmas Wish

Cowboy Angel in Disguise

Cowboy Foreman in Love

Cowboy Blind Date Mix-Up

Cowboy On-the-Job Boyfriend

Cowboy Single Dad Crush

Cowboy Grumpy Boss

Cowboy Friend Zone

Cowboy Stolen Kiss

Cowboy Accidentally Hitched

Born in Texas: Hometown Heroes A=Z

Accidental Hero

Best Friend Hero

Celebrity Hero

Damaged Hero

Enemies to Hero

Forbidden Hero

Guardian Hero

Hunk and Hero

Instantly Her Hero

Jilted Hero

Kissable Hero

Long Distance Hero

Mistaken Hero

Not Good Enough Hero

Opposites Attract Hero

PenPal Hero

Texas Hotline

The Plus One Hero

The Secret Baby Hero

The Bridesmaid Hero

The Girl Next Door Hero

The Secret Crush Hero

The Bachelorette Hero

The Rebound Hero

The Fake Bride Hero

The Blind Date Hero

The Maid by Mistake Hero

The Unlucky Bride Hero

The Temporary Family Hero

Black Tie Billionaires

Her Billionaire Boss

Her Billionaire Bodyguard

Her Billionaire Secret Admirer

Her Billionaire Best Friend

Her Billionaire Geek

Her Billionaire Double Date

Heart Lake

Winds of Change

Song of Nightingales

Perils of Starlight

Return of Miracles

Thousands of Gifts

Race of Champions

Storm of Secrets

Season of Angels

Clash of Hearts

Mountain of Fire

Night of Mercy

Echoes of Home

Cowboy Confessions

Mr. Not Right for Her

Mr. Maybe Right for Her

Mr. Right But She Doesn't Know It

Mr. Right Again for Her

Mr. Yeah, Right. As If…

Texas Billionaires

Her Billionaire's Birthday Date

Her Billionaire's Birthday Blind Date

Her Billionaire's Birthday Secret

❄

For a printable list of my books:

Tap here

or go to:

https://www.JoGrafford.com/books

For a printable list of my Jovie Grace books *(sweet historical romance)*:

Tap here

or go to:

https://www.jografford.com/joviegracebooks

Made in United States
North Haven, CT
23 August 2024